[handwritten signatures/inscription:] Best Marci
Jamie (?)
(?) Paddock
Sidney Thompson
Suzanne Hud(?)

[barcode] D0989222

THE ALUMNI GRILL

Edited by

William Gay and Suzanne Kingsbury

MacAdam/Cage
155 Sansome Street, Suite 550
San Francisco, CA 94104
www.macadamcage.com
Copyright © 2004
ALL RIGHTS RESERVED.

The Alumni Grill / edited by Suzanne Kingsbury and William Gay.
    p. cm.
    ISBN 1-931561-79-6 (alk. paper)
    1. Southern States—Social life and customs—Fiction. 2. Short stories, American—Southern States. I. Kingsbury, Suzanne. II. Gay, William.
    PS551.A45 2004
    810.8'0975—dc22

2004014217

Manufactured in the United States of America.
10 9 8 7 6 5 4 3 2 1

Book and cover design by Dorothy Carico Smith.

Several of these stories have appeared elsewhere, in some cases in a different form:
"Christians" by Tom Franklin in *Hell at the Breech* (Perennial, 2003); "Smash & Grab" by Michael Knight in *StoryQuarterly* #39 (Fall 2003); "Fleet's Eats: Tales of the Culinary Underground" by John T. Edge in *The Oxford American*; "Down the Shore Everything is All Right" by Michelle Richmond in *Glimmer Train* #41 and *The Girl in the Fall-Away Dress* (University of Massachusetts Press, 2001); "Daddy Phase," "Lo, the Child Displayeth Cunning, Paradise is Fayling," "Waiting for the Heart to Moderate," "Making an Egg for Claire, Sunny-side Up" and "The Gods Tell Me, You Will Forget All This" by Beth Ann Fennelly in *Tender Hooks* (W. W. Norton & Co., 2004); "The Warsaw Voice" by Steve Yarbrough in the *Tampa Review* (Spring 1995) and *Veneer* (University of Missouri Press, 1998); "La Prade" by Suzanne Hudson in *Penthouse* (1997) and *Opposable Thumbs* (Livingston University Press, 2001); "White Trash Fishing" by Ron Rash in the *Raleigh News and Observer*; "The Ones Who Are Holding Things Up" by Jennifer Paddock in *A Secret Word* (Touchstone/Simon & Schuster, 2004); "Cavity Star" by Jamie Kornegay in *Oxford Town* (August 7-14, 1997); "Floating" by Sidney Thompson in *The Southern Review* (Winter 2002, Vol. 38, No. 1); "The Cool of the Day" by Silas House in *Bayou Magazine* (issue 41, 2003); "Handcuffed" by Bev Marshall in *Potpourri: A Magazine of the Literary Arts* (Vol. 9. No. 2 1997); "Water Dog God" by Brad Watson in *The Oxford American* (1999).

Publisher's note: This is a work of fiction. Names, characters, places, and incidents either are the product of the author's imagination or are used fictitiously. Any resemblance to actual events, locales, or persons, living or dead, is entirely coincidental.

THE ALUMNI GRILL

Edited by

William Gay and Suzanne Kingsbury

MacAdam/Cage

TABLE OF CONTENTS

For Sonny

ACKNOWLEDGMENTS

The editors would like to thank the authors for their hard work and stunning prose. May they be anthologized and loved for years to come.

Thank you also to everyone at MacAdam/Cage—especially Kate Nitze, Pat Walsh, and the royal emperor of the *Blue Moon Café* series, David Poindexter.

Introduction

Why not weep when we read? Why not laugh? Why not taste summer wind in winter? Wail with pleasure? Forget this world? You are sixteen again and taking risks, denying yourself nothing. This book allows soaring moments where you enter a Narnia adept at perfect escape.

In 2002 Sonny Brewer, an infamous bearded bookstore owner from Fairhope, Alabama, began the *Blue Moon Café* anthology. The second edition came out in 2003. Sonny is a Saint Nick incarnate. He makes dreams come true; he gifts the world literary treasure. He is perhaps the only one who could have brought these writers together. He hand-chose the golden quills that filled those books' pages, and readers rejoiced. Writers of all ilk and manner flooded the bounded volumes of prose, flush with talent. Readers responded by coming from distant counties to listen to these literary legends of the South. Thirty-eight writers of powerful Southern prose combined humor and startling depth, traveling distances through kudzu and cotton-marked highways where their fans met them to bear witness to the reading of their work. These authors gathered crowds wherever they went, creating audiences in Fairhope, Alabama, Oxford,

Mississippi, Nashville, Tennessee.

They are again gathered here in prose not printed in the other two anthologies. In this book, you are availed by the seasoned veterans, the lovers of the story, excerpt, and poem. They will drown you in the puissance of their words. Their banquet of worlds has an intensity of expression sometimes kin to the power and terror of Armageddon and other times moving you to teenage laughter.

Enter here the fictional forgotten voices of the South. Beginning with the mother and lover of Tom Franklin's murderers, and her final offering of redemption, and ending with the thinly clad half-feral figure of Brad Watson's pregnant girl, emerging to her savior from an incestuous past. In between we read John T. Edge's love of the food that satisfies the Southern palate, the sexual and matronly body of Beth Ann Fennelly's poetry, Bev Marshall's deftly drawn housewife, secretly fascinated by an escaped rapist at large in her suburban neighborhood, the Southern fishing described in humorous and stunning detail by award-winning writer Ron Rash and the Poland of Steve Yarbrough. Silas House brings you the lost love between two couples and a balmy night, beautiful but fraught with melancholy. Jennifer Paddock makes us remember high school in vivid clarity. Suzanne Hudson's story about a teenage daughter-now-mother surviving in backcountry Mississippi with a deranged father won a contest judged by the likes of Kurt Vonnegut and Toni Morrison and has been reprinted here after its debut thirty-four years ago.

Where are you now? Out of your own world and into a world rich with vitality, with desire and sometimes death and nostalgic love. Scribing so utterly human it will stay with you long after you have finished the last page.

Let their work be a beating, beautiful beast that fills you, so you are sensual and divine, naughty and deep. These stories are grave markers where you stop and re-member and again lift the stone and again are rebirthed. We are talking about immortality and what better reason to be alive? You are swallowed whole. Enjoy.

Suzanne Kingsbury

CHRISTIANS
Tom Franklin

1887

It was August, so she had to bury him quick. Soon she would be able to smell him, a thing she didn't know if she could endure—not the live, biting odor he brought in from a day in the fields but a mixture of turned earth and rot, an odor she associated with decaying possum and coon carcasses, the bowl of a turtle she'd overturned as a girl and then tumbled away from, vomiting at the soup of maggots pulsing inside.

It was late afternoon. He lay on his back on the porch, covered by a sheet stained across the torso with blood, the sheet mapped with flies and more coming, as many flies as she'd seen gathered in one place, a revival of them, death calling like the holy spirit. In her left hand she held his hat, which the two men had thrown to the ground after they'd rolled him off the wagon, the impact setting him to bleeding afresh.

She hadn't wailed at the sight. Hadn't flung herself on the body or swiped her fingernails at their implacable faces as they watched, the two of them, one young, one old. She hadn't even put her hand over her mouth.

They told her they'd kept his gun. Said they meant to give it to the sheriff. Said like father like son.

"Leave," is all she'd said.

And she herself had dragged him up the steps, holding him under his arms. She herself had draped him with their spare bed sheet and turned her rocking chair east to face him and sit rocking. The bloodstain had quit spreading and she gazed past him—past the corpse of him and its continents of flies—to the outreaching cotton so stark and white in the sun she could barely look at it, cotton she'd have to pick herself now that her son was dead.

*

Sheriff Waite came. He got down off his horse and left the reins hanging and stood in the yard. He studied the drag marks, the stained dirt. His green eyes followed the marks and paused at the blood on the plank steps and the gritty line of blood smeared across the porch. He watched the boy under the sheet for nearly a minute before he moved his eyes—it seemed such an effort for him to look at country folks—to her face. In the past she'd always had trouble meeting town men's eyes, the lust there or the judgment, but now she sat rocking and staring back at him as though she understood a secret about him not even his wife knew. His hand went up toward his nose, an unconscious gesture, as if he'd cover it, but he must've considered it improper or disrespectful—despite the dead being a sharecropper—for he lowered the hand and cleared his throat.

"Missus Freemont."

"It was that Glaine Bolton," she said. "Him and Marcus

Eady."

Waite stepped closer to the porch. Behind him his tall handsome horse had sweat tracks leading down through the dust caked on its coat. It wiggled its long head and blinked and sighed at the heat, flicked the skin of its back so that the saddle moved and moved the rifle standing in its scabbard.

"I know who it was," Waite said. "They done already come talked to me. Caught me over at Coffeeville." He moved his hand again, as if he didn't know what to do with it without the weight of a gun in it. "How I was able to get here so quick."

She folded her arms despite the heat, nestled her sweating breasts between them.

"They give me his pistol," Waite said, but she didn't see it on him.

She waited, and his face seemed to become all lines as he got himself ready to say out loud what she knew already. That there would be no justice. Not the kind she wanted, anyway. Since it was so easy to look at him now, she did it, reckoning him in his late forties. If she hadn't been so brimming with hate, she'd have still considered him fine-looking, even all these years later. His shirt fit well at the shoulders, his pants snug at the hips. He was skinnier than before. One thing she noticed was that his fingers weren't scarred from cotton, where nail met skin, the way hers and her son's were. Had been.

"You see," he began, "it's pretty generally known where your boy was going." He flapped a hand at her son. "When they stopped him."

"Stopped him? That's what you call what they done?"

"Yes'm."

She waited.

"He was going to shoot Glaine's daddy."

She waited. She realized she'd quit rocking and pushed at the porch boards with her bare feet until she was moving again, whisper of wind on the back of her neck, beneath her bun of brown hair. She heard her breath going in and out of her nose.

Waite suddenly took off his hat and began to examine the brim, the leather band sweated through, then turned it over and looked into the dark crown shaped by his head. "Way I hear it," he said, "is your boy and Travis Bolton had some words at the Coffeeville Methodist last week. I wasn't there, see. I'd been serving a warrant down in Jackson."

When Waite came forward she heard his holster creak. He set a foot on the bottom step, careful not to touch the dark brown dried blood, and bent at the waist and rested his elbows on his knee, still intent on the hat. "But I got me a long memory, Missus Freemont. And the thing I told you back then, well, it still stands."

*

Bess had a long memory, too.

She'd been sixteen years younger. Sixteen years younger and almost asleep when that wagon had rattled up outside. She'd risen from where she'd been kneeling before the hearth, half in prayer, half for warmth. Another cold December day had passed, she remembered, rain coming, or snow. It was dark out, windy at intervals, the rocking chair on the porch tapping against the front wall. A pair of sweet potatoes on the rocks before her all the food they had left.

A horse nickered. She pulled her shawl around her

shoulders and held it at her throat. Clay, not two years old then, had been asleep under a quilt on the floor beside her. Now he got up.

"Stay here, boy," she told him, resting a hand on top of his head. He wore a tattered shirt and pants given by church women from the last county they'd lived in, just over a week before. Barefooted, he stood shivering with his back to the fire, hands behind him, the way his father liked to stand.

On the porch, she pulled the latch closed behind her and peered into the weakly starred night. Movement. Then a lantern rose and a man in a duster coat and derby hat seemed to form out of the fabric of darkness. He wore a beard and spectacles that reflected the light he held above him.

"Would you tell me your name, Miss?" he asked her.

She said it, her knuckles cold at her throat. She heard the door open behind her and stepped in front of it to shield Clay.

"This is my land you're on," the man said, "and that's one of my tenant houses y'all are camped out in."

Bess felt relief. *He's only here about the property.*

"My husband," she said. "He ain't home."

"Miss," the man said, "I believe I know that."

Fear again. She came forward on the porch, boards loose beneath her feet, and stopped on the first step. The horse shook its head and stamped against the cold. "Easy," the man whispered. He set the brake and stepped from the seat into the back of the wagon, holding the lantern aloft. He bent and began pushing something heavy. Bess came down the first step. Behind her, Clay slipped out the door.

The man climbed from the tailgate of the wagon and

took a few steps toward her. He was shorter than she was, even with his hat and in his boots. Now she could see his eyes.

"My name is Mister Bolton," he said. "Could you walk over here, Miss?"

She seemed unable to move. The dirt was cold, her toes numb. He waited a moment, gazing past her at Clay. Then he looked down, shaking his head. He came toward her and she recoiled as if he might hit her, but he only placed a gloved hand on her back and pushed her forward, not roughly but firmly. They went that way to the wagon, where she looked in and, in the light of his lantern, saw her husband.

E. J. was dead. His jacket opened and his shirtfront red with blood. His fingers were squeezed into fists and his head thrown back, mouth opened. His hair covered his eyes.

"He was stealing from me," Bolton said. "I seen somebody down in my smokehouse and thought it was a nigger. I yelled at him to stop but he took off running."

"Stealing what?" she asked, her voice small.

"A ham," Bolton said.

Bess's knees began to give way, she grasped the wagon edge. Her shawl fell off and she stood in her thin dress. Bolton steadied her, his arm going around her shoulders. He set the lantern on the floor of the wagon, by E. J.'s boot.

"I am sorry, Miss," Bolton said, a hand now at each of her shoulders. "I wish...."

Clay had appeared behind her, hugging himself, his toes curling in the dirt.

"Go on in, boy," she told him. "Now."

He didn't move.

"Do like your momma says," Bolton ordered, and Clay

turned and ran up the stairs and went inside, pulling the door to.

Bolton led Bess back to the porch and she slumped on the steps. He retrieved her shawl and hung it across her shoulders.

"My own blame fault," he said. "I knew y'all was out here. Just ain't had time to come see you. Run you off."

No longer able to hold back, Bess was sobbing into her hands, which smelled of smoke. Some fraction of her, she knew, was glad E. J. was gone, glad he'd no longer pull them from place to place only to be threatened off at gunpoint by some landowner again and again. No more of the sudden rages or the beatings he gave her or Clay or some bystander. But, she thought, for all his violence, there were the nights he got only half-drunk and they slept enmeshed in each other's limbs, her gown up high where she'd pulled it and his long johns around one ankle. His quiet snoring. The marvelous lightness between her legs and the mattress wet beneath them. There were those nights. And there was the boy, her darling son, who needed a stern hand, a father, even if what he got was one like E. J., prone to temper and meanness when he drank too much whiskey. Where would they go now, she asked herself, the two of them?

"Miss?" Bolton tugged at his beard.

She looked up. It had begun to rain, cold drops on her face, in her eyes.

"You want me to leave him here?" Bolton asked her. "I don't know what else to do with him. I'll go fetch the sheriff directly. He'll ride out tomorrow, I expect."

"Yeah," Bess said. She blinked. "Would you wait...?" She looked toward the window where Clay's face ducked out of sight.

"Go on ahead," he said.

Inside, she told the boy to take his quilt into the next room and wait for her.

When she came out, Bolton was wrestling E. J. to the edge of the wagon. Bess helped him and together they dragged him up the steps.

"You want to leave him on the porch?" Bolton huffed. "He'll keep better."

"No," she said. "Inside."

He looked doubtful but helped her pull him into the house. They rolled him over on a torn sheet on the floor by the hearth. In the soft flickering firelight, her husband seemed somehow even more dead, a ghost, the way the shadows moved on his still features, his flat nose, the dark hollows under his eyes that Clay would likely have as well. She pushed his hair back. She touched his lower jaw and closed his mouth. Tried to remember the last thing he'd said to her when he left that afternoon but couldn't. His mouth slowly fell back open, and she put one of the sweet potatoes under his chin as a prop.

Bolton was gazing around the room, still wearing his gloves, hands on his hips. Abruptly, he walked across the floor and went outside, closing the door behind him. When he came back in, she jumped up and stared at him.

In one arm he held a bundle.

"This is the ham," he said, casting about for somewhere to set it. When nowhere seemed right, he knelt and laid it beside the door. "Reckon it's paid for."

He waited a few moments, his breath misting, then went outside, shutting the door. She heard it latch. Heard the wagon's brake released and the creak of hinges and

the horse whinny and stamp and the wheels click as Mr.
Bolton rolled off into the night. She went to the window
and outside was only darkness. She turned.

Her fingers trembling, Bess unwrapped the cloth sack
from around the ham, a good ten-pounder, the bone still
in it. A pang of guilt turned in her chest when her mouth
watered. Already its smoked smell filled the tiny room. She
touched the cold, hard surface, saw four strange pock-
marks in its red skin. Horrified, she used a fingernail to dig
out a pellet of buckshot. It dropped and rolled over the uneven floor. She looked at her husband's bloody shirt.

"Oh, E. J.," she whispered.

The next morning, as Bolton predicted, Waite had arrived. She'd left Clay in the back, eating ham with his fingers.

"I'm the Sheriff," he said, walking past her into the
cold front room. He didn't take off his hat. His cheeks
were clean-shaven and red from wind and he wore a red
mustache with the ends twisted into tiny waxed tips. The
silver star pinned to his shirt was askew, its topmost point
aimed at his left shoulder.

Moving through the room, looking in the corners and
at the floor, everywhere except at the body of her husband, he seemed angry. When he saw E. J.'s old single-
barrel shotgun he took it up from the corner where it
stood and unbreeched it and removed the shell and
dropped it in his pocket. He snapped the gun closed and
replaced it. The door to the back room was shut, and
glancing her way, he pushed aside his coat to reveal the
white wood handle of a sidearm on his gunbelt. Pistol in
hand, he eased open the door and peered in. The little
boy he saw must not have seemed threatening because he
closed the door and holstered his pistol. He brushed past

Bess where she stood by the window and clopped in his boots to the hearth and squatted by E. J. and studied him. He patted the dead man's pockets, withdrew a plug of tobacco and set it on the hearth stones.

Watching, she felt a sting of anger at E. J., buying tobacco when the boy needed feeding. In E. J.'s right boot the sheriff found the knife her husband always carried. He glanced at her and laid it on the rocks beside the plug but found nothing else.

Waite squatted a moment longer, as if considering the height and weight of the dead man, then rose and stepped past the body to be closer to her. He cleared his throat and asked where they'd come from. She told him. Tennessee. He asked how long they'd been here illegally on Mr. Bolton's property and she told him that, too. Then he asked what she planned to do now.

She said, "I don't know."

Then she said, "I want my husband's pistol back. And that shotgun shell, too."

"That's a bold request," he said. "For someone in your position."

"My 'position.'"

"Trespasser. Mr. Bolton shot a thief. There are those would argue that sidearm belongs to him now."

Unable to meet his eyes, she glared at his boots. Muddied at the tips, along the heels.

"I'll leave the shell when I go," he said, "but I won't have a loaded gun while I'm here."

"You think I'd shoot you?"

"No, I don't. But you won't get the chance. The undertaker will be here directly. I passed him back yonder at the bridge."

"I can't afford no undertaker."

"Mr. Bolton's already paid him."

Bess felt her cheeks redden. "I don't understand."

"Ma'am," he said, folding his arms, "the fact is, some of us has too little conscience, and some has too much." He raised his chin to indicate E. J. "I expect your husband yonder chose the right man to try and rob."

She refused to cry. She folded her arms over her chest and wished the shawl could swallow her whole.

"I have but one piece of advice for you," the sheriff said, lowering his voice, "and you should take it. Travis Bolton is a damned good man. I've known him for over ten years. If I was you I would get the hell out of this county. And wherever it is you end up, I wouldn't tell that young one of yours who pulled the trigger on his daddy. Cause if this thing goes any farther, even if it's ten years from now, fifteen, twenty years, I'll be the one that ends it." He had looked at E. J. as he might look at a slop jar, then turned to go.

From the window, she'd watched him toss the shotgun shell onto the frozen dirt and swing into his saddle and spur his horse to a trot, as if he couldn't get away from such business fast enough. From such people.

*

"Travis Bolton's a good man," Waite repeated now, putting his hat back on. "And it ain't that he's my wife's brother. Which I reckon you know. And it ain't that he's turned into a preacher, neither. If he needed hanging, I'd do it. Hanged a preacher in Dickinson one time, least he said he was a preacher. Didn't stop him from stealing horses. Hanged my second cousin's oldest boy once, too.

A murderer, that one. Duty's a thing I ain't never shied from, is what I'm saying. And what I said back then, in case you've forgot, is that you better not tell that boy who killed his daddy. Cause if you do, he'll be bound to avengement."

"Wasn't me told him," she said. So quietly he had to lean in and ask her to repeat herself, which she did.

"Who told him, then?"

"The preacher's son his self did."

Waite straightened, his arms dangling. Fingers flexing. He looked at her dead boy. He looked back at her. "Well, Glaine ain't the man his daddy is. I'm first to admit that. Preacher's sons," he said, but didn't finish.

"Told him at school, Sheriff. Walked up to my boy in the schoolyard and said, 'My daddy kilt your daddy, what'll you say about that, trash.' It was five years ago, it happened. When my boy wasn't but thirteen years old. Five years he had to live with that knowing, and do nothing. Five years I was able to keep him from doing something. And all the time that Glaine Bolton looking at him like he was a coward. Him and that whole bunch of boys from town."

Waite took off his hat again. Flies had drifted over and he swatted at them. He rubbed a finger under his nose, along his mustache that was going gray. "Thing is, Missus Freemont, that there ain't against the law. Young fellows being mean. It ain't fair, it ain't right, but it ain't illegal, either. What is illegal is your boy taking up that Colt that I never should've give you back and waving it around at the church like I heard he done last Sunday. Threatening everbody. Saying he was gone kill the man killed his daddy, even if he is a preacher."

Last Sunday, yes. He'd gone out before dawn without telling her. Soon as she'd awakened to such an empty house, soon as she opened the drawer where they kept the pistol and saw nothing but her needle and thread there, the box of cartridges gone too, she'd known. Known. But then he'd come home, come home and said no, he didn't kill nobody, you have to be a man to kill somebody, and he reckoned all he was was a coward, like everybody said.

Thank God, she'd whispered, hugging him.

Waite dug a handkerchief from his back pocket and wiped his forehead. "Only thing I wish," he said, "is that somebody'd come told me. If somebody had, I'd have rode out and got him myself. Put him in jail a spell, tried to talk some sense into him. Told him all killing Bolton'd do is get him hanged. Or shot one. But nobody warned me. You yourself didn't come tell me. Travis, neither. And I'm just a fellow by his self with a lot of county to mind. One river to the other. Why I count on folks to help me. Tell me things."

He looked again at her son, shook his head. "If he'd had a daddy, might've been a different end. You don't know. But when a fellow says—in hearing of a lot of witnesses, mind you—that he's gone walk to a man's house and shoot him, well, that's enough cause for Glaine Bolton and Marcus Eady to take up a post in the bushes and wait. I'd have done the same thing myself, you want the truth. And if your boy come along, toting that pistol, heading up toward my house, well ma'am, I'd a shot him too."

A fly landed on her arm, tickle of its air-light feet over her skin. Waite said other things but she never again looked up at him and didn't answer him further or take notice when he sighed one last time and turned and gathered the reins of his mount and climbed on the animal's back and sat a spell longer and then finally prodded the horse with his spurs and walked it away.

She sat watching her hands. There was dried blood on her knuckles, beneath her nails, that she wouldn't ever wash off. Blood on her dress front. She'd have to bury her boy now, and this time there'd be no undertaker to summon the preacher so it could be a Christian funeral. She'd have to find the preacher herself. This time there was only her.

*

She walked two miles along unfenced cotton fields wearing Clay's hat, which had been E.J.'s before Clay took it up. She didn't see a person the whole time. She saw a treeful of crows, spiteful loud things that didn't fly as she passed, and a possum that waddled across the road behind her, making her turn at its scratching noises over the dirt. She carried her family Bible. For no reason she could name she remembered a school spelling bee she'd almost won, except the word "Bible" had caused her to lose. She'd not said, "Capital 'B,'" to begin the word, had just recited its letters so her teacher had disqualified her. Someone else got the ribbon.

Her Bible was sweaty from her hand so she switched it to the other hand then carried it up under her arm for awhile. Later she read in it as she walked, to pass the time, from her favorite book, Judges.

Her pastor, Brother Hill, lived with his wife and eight daughters in a four-room house at a bend in the road. Like everyone else, they grew cotton. With eight sets of extra hands, they did well at it, and the blonde stepping-stone girls, less than a year apart and all blue-eyed like their father, were marvels of efficiency in the field, tough and uncomplaining children. For Bess it was a constant struggle not to covet the preacher and his family. She liked his wife, too, a tiny woman named Elda, and more than once had had to ask God's forgiveness for picturing herself in Elda's frilly blue town dress and bonnet with a pair of blonde girls, the youngest two, holding each of her hands as the group of them crossed the street in Coffeeville on a Saturday. And once—more than once—she'd imagined herself to be Elda in the sanctity of the marriage bed. Then rolling into her own stale pillow which took her tears and her repentance. How understanding God was said to be, and yet how little understanding she had witnessed. Even He, even God, had only sacrificed once.

Girls. Everyone thought them the lesser result. The lesser sex. But to Bess a girl was something that didn't have to pick up his daddy's pistol out of the sideboard and ignore his mother's crying and push her away and leave her on the floor as he opened the door checking the pistol's loads. Looking back looking just like his daddy in his daddy's hat. A girl was something that didn't run down the road and leap sideways into the tall cotton and disappear like a deer in order to get away and leave you alone in the yard, trying to pull your fingers out of their sockets.

She stopped in the heat atop a high place in the road. She looked behind her and saw no one. Just the cotton. In front of her, the same. Grasshoppers springing through the air and for noise only bird whistles and the distant razz of cicadas. She looked at her Bible and raised it to throw it into the cotton. For a long time she stood in this pose, but it was only a pose, which God saw or didn't, and after a time she lowered her arm and walked on.

*

At Brother Hill's some of his girls were shelling peas on the porch. Others were shucking corn, saving the husks in a basket. Things a family did while the cotton was laid by. When they saw her coming along the fence, one hopped up and went inside and returned with her mother. Bess stopped, tried in a half-panic to remember each girl's name but could only recall four or five. Elda stood on the steps with her hand leveled over her eyes like the brim of a hat, squinting to see. When Bess didn't move, Elda came down the steps toward her, stopping at the well for a tin cup of water, leaving the shadow of her house to meet Bess so the girls wouldn't hear what they were going to say.

"Dear, I'm so sorry," Elda whispered when Bess had finished. She reached to trace a finger down Bess's face. She offered the tin which Bess drank quickly and gave back.

"I thank you," she said, moving the Bible from one hand to the other.

Elda reached and held her empty hand, squeezed her fingers. "Will you stay to supper with us? Let us go over and help you prepare him? I can set up with you. Me and my oldest."

Bess shook her head. "I can get him ready myself. I only came to see if Brother Hill would read the service."

The watchful girls resumed work, like a picture come suddenly alive, when their mother looked back toward them.

"Oh, dear," Elda said. "He's away. His first cousin died in Grove Hill and he's there doing that service. He won't be back until day after tomorrow, in time for picking. Can you wait, dear?"

She said she couldn't, the heat was too much. She'd find someone else, another preacher. Even if he wasn't a Baptist.

*

It was after dark when she arrived at the next place, a dog-trot house with a mule standing in the trot. There was a barn off in the shadows down the sloping land and the chatter of chickens everywhere. This man was a Methodist from Hattiesburg, Mississippi, but he was prone to fits and was in the midst of one then, his wife said, offering Bess a cup of water and a biscuit which she took but didn't eat. Though Bess couldn't recall her name, she knew that here was a good woman who'd married the minister after her sister, his first wife, had died of malaria. Been a mother to the children.

In a whisper, casting a glance at the house, the woman told Bess that her husband hadn't been himself for nearly a week and showed no sign of returning to his natural, caring state. She'd sent the young ones to a neighbor's.

As Bess walked away, she heard him moaning from inside and calling out profane words. A hand seemed to clamp her neck and she felt suddenly cold though her dress was soaked with sweat. God above was nothing if not a giver of tests. When she thought to look for it, the biscuit was gone, she'd dropped it somewhere.

The last place to go was to the nigger preacher, but she didn't do that. She walked toward home instead and thought she smelled him on the wind on her face before she came in sight of their house. For a long time she sat on the porch holding his cold hand in hers, held it for so long it grew warm from her warmth, and for a spell she imagined he was alive, sleeping. The flies had gone wherever flies go after dark and she fell asleep, praying.

She woke against the wall with a pain in her neck like an iron in it. The flies were back. She gasped at their

number and fell off the porch batting them away. In the
yard was a pair of wild dogs that she chased down the road
with a hoe. There were buzzards smudged against the
white sky, mocking things that may have been from God or
the devil, she had no idea which. One seemed the same as
the other to her now as she got to her knees.

Got to her knees and pushed him and pulled him inside and lay over him crying. With more strength than she
knew she possessed, she lifted him onto the sideboard and
stood bent and panting. He was tall so his ankles and feet
stuck out in the air. She waved both hands at the flies but
most were outside, only a few had got in. She closed the
door, the shutters, and moved back the sheet to look at his
face. For a moment it was E. J. she saw. Then it wasn't. She
touched Clay's chin, rasp of whisker. It was only a year he'd
been shaving. She built a little fire in the stove, heated
some water, found the straight razor and soaped his cold
face. A fly flew out of his mouth. She scraped the razor over
his cheeks, rubbing the stiff hairs onto the sheet that still
covered his body, her hand on his neck, thumb caressing
his Adam's apple. She talked to him as she shaved him and
talked to him as she peeled back the stiff sheet and unlaced
his brogans and set them side by side on the floor. She had
never prepared anyone for burial and wished Elda were
here and told him this in a quiet voice, but then added that
she'd not want anybody to see him in such a state, especially since she'd imagined that he and Elda's oldest
daughter would someday be wed. Or the second oldest.
You could've had your pick of them, she said.

We would've all spent Christmases together in their
house and the sound of a baby laughing would be the
sound of music to my ears. His clothes stank, so she unfas-

tened his work pants and told him she'd launder them as she inched them over his hips, his knees, ankles. She removed his underpants which were soiled and covered his privates with the sheet from her bed. She unbuttoned his shirt and spread it and closed her eyes then opened them to look at the wounds. Each near his heart. Two eye-socket holes—she could cover them with one hand and knew enough about shooting to note the skill of the marksman—the skin black around them. She flecked the hardened blood away with her fingernails and washed him with soap and water that turned pink on his skin. Doing his back was messier as one of the bullets had come out and taken much of him with them, and in the end she had to stuff a rag in to close him up. Then, with his middle covered, she washed him and combed his hair. She had been talking the entire time. Now she stopped.

She snatched off the sheet and beheld her boy, naked as the day he'd wriggled into the world of air and men. It was time for him to go home and she began to cry again. "Look what they did," she said.

*

The Reverend Isaiah Hovington Walker's place seemed deserted. The house was painted white, which had upset many of the white people in the area, that a nigger man would have the gall to doctor up his house so that it no longer had that hornet's nest gray wood the rest of the places in these parts had. He'd even painted his outhouse, which had nearly got him lynched. So many of the white folks, Bess and Clay included, not having privies themselves. If Sheriff Waite hadn't come out and made him scrape off the outhouse paint (at gunpoint, she'd heard), there'd have been one less preacher for her to consult today.

"Isaiah Walker," she called. "Get on out here."

Three short-haired yellow dogs kept her at the edge of the yard while she waited, her neck still throbbing from the crick in it. She watched the windows, curtains pulled, for a sign of movement. She looked over at the well, its bucket and rope, longing for a sup of water, but it wouldn't do for her to drink here. "Isaiah Walker," she called again, remembering how, on their first night in the area, E. J. had horse-whipped Walker for not getting his mule off the road fast enough. Though the preacher had kicked and pulled the mule's halter until his hands were bloody, E. J. had muttered that a nigger's mule ought to have as much respect for its betters as the nigger himself. He'd snatched the wagon's brake and drawn from its holder the stiff whip. She'd hoped it was the mule he meant to hit, but it hadn't been.

The dogs were inching toward her, hackles flashing over their backs, taking their courage from each other, smelling the blood on her hands, her dress. She wished she'd brought a stick with her. She'd even left her Bible this time, saw it in her mind's eye as it lay splayed open on the porch with the wind paging it. She hadn't eaten since they'd brought Clay back, and for a moment she thought she might faint. But she wouldn't leave.

She stamped at the dogs and they stopped their approach but kept barking. Still, it must have been half an hour before Walker's door finally opened, the dogs never having stopped. She lowered her hand from her neck. The reverend came out fastening his suspenders and put a toothpick in his mouth. He looked up at the sky as if seeking rain. A man entirely bald of hair but with a long white beard and white eyebrows and small rifle-barrel eyes. He whistled at the dogs but they ignored him and ignored him when he called them by name.

She thought it proper for him to come down and meet her, but he never left the porch.

"This how you treat white folks?" she croaked at him.

"I know you," he said at last. "Heard why you here, too. And you might try tell me the Lord God, He expect me to forgive. But I been in there praying since you first step in my yard, Missus Freemont, since them dogs first start they racket, and I been intent on listen what God say. But He ain't say nothing 'bout me saying no words over your boy soul. If He wanted me to, He'd a said so. Might be them dogs stop barking. That would tell me. The Lord, He ain't never been shy 'bout telling me what to do and I ain't never been shy 'bout listening."

But she had turned away before he'd finished, and by the time the dogs stopped their noise she had rounded a curve and gone up a hill and then sat in the road and then lay in it.

Lay in it thinking of her young life, of her farmer father, widowed and quick to punish, overburdened with his failing tobacco farm and seven children, she the second oldest and a dreamer of daydreams, possessed he said by the demon Sloth. Of the narrow-shouldered, handsome man coming on horseback seemingly from between the round mountains she'd seen and not seen all her life, galloping she thought right down out of the broad purple sky onto her father's property. The young man taking one look at her and campaigning and working and coercing and at last trading her father that fine black mare for a battered wagon, a pair of mules and a thin eighteen-year-old wife glad to see someplace new. Of crossing steaming green Tennessee in the wagon, of clear cool rainless nights with the canvas top drawn aside, lying shoulder to shoulder with her husband, the sky huge and intense overhead, stars winking past on their distant, pre-told trajectories, the mules braying down by the creek where they were staked and she falling asleep smelling their dying fire, his arms around her.

E. J. Ezekiel Jeremiah. No living person knows what them letters stands for but you, he'd said.

Ezekiel, she'd repeated. Jeremiah.

Out of the wagon to jump across the state line (which he'd drawn in the dirt with his shoe), laughing, holding hands, and going south through so much Alabama she thought it must spread all the way from Heaven to Hell. Slate mountains gave way to flatland and swamp to red clay hills, and they ferried a wide river dead as glass then bumped over dry stony roads atop the buckboard pulled by the two thinning mules. Then the older mule died: within two months of their wedding.

E. J. not saying anything, for a long time, staring at the carcass where it lay in the field, hands on his hips, his back to her; and then saying why the hell didn't she tell him her daddy was trading a bum mule.

For days and mostly in silence they paralleled a lonely railroad until it just stopped and there were nigger men hammering alongside white ones and the ring of metal on metal and tents speckling the horizon and octoroon whores hanging their stockings on what looked to be a traveling gallows.

For two months he laid crossties and flirted (and

more) with the whores. Then they departed on a Sunday at dawn when he was still drunk from the night. She had a high fever and from inside her hot lolling head it seemed they were slipping off the land, ever southward into an ooze of mud.

Then clabbertrap railroad or river towns on the landscape, she expecting a baby and sick each afternoon, staying with the wagon and reading in her Bible while he walked in or rode aback the remaining mule to find a game of blackjack or stud and coming out more often than not with less money than he'd gone in with, her little dowry smaller and smaller and then things traded, the iron skillet from her grandmother for groceries and her uncle's fiddle—which she could play a little—for cartridges. E. J. had begun to sleep with the pistol by his head and his arms around his coat, the wagon always covered at night now, as if he'd deny her the stars. Waking one morning to a world shelled in bright snow and that evening giving birth to the squalling boy they called Clay, after her father who, despite herself, she missed.

Where we going? she'd asked E. J. and he'd said, To a place I know of.

Which, eventually, was here. The cabin that belonged to Travis Bolton. Who lived in a large house four miles away and who killed E. J. for a ham and then said she and Clay could stay on in the cabin, if they wanted to, and not pay rent, and pick cotton for him when harvest time came.

Some thoughtful part of her knew it was killing E. J. that had let Travis Bolton hear God's call. That made him do whatever a man did, within his heart and without—papers, vows—to become a preacher of the gospel. She imagined him a man of extravagant gestures, who when

he gave himself to Christ gave fully and so not only allowed her and her boy to work and live on his land, in his
house, but did more. On the coldest days she might find a
gutted doe laid across the wood that had once been a
fence at the edge of the property. Or a plucked turkey at
Christmas. Not a month after E. J. had been committed to
the earth by Brother Hill, a milk cow had shown up with
the Bolton brand on it. She'd waited for Mr. Bolton or his
hand Marcus Eady to come claim it, but after a day and a
night no one had and so she'd sheltered it in the lean-to
back of the house. Aware she could be called a thief, she'd
wrapped Clay in E. J.'s coat (buckshot holes still in it) and
carried him to the Bolton place. Instinct sent her to the
back door where a nigger woman eyed her down a broad
nose and went fetched Mrs. Bolton who told her Mr.
Bolton meant for her to use the cow so that the boy might
have milk. And while part of Bess understood certain
things about Travis Bolton's choices, there was another
part of her too, a listening, observing part, and this part
discerned that Mrs. Bolton disapproved of her husband's
decision to let the squatters stay out there in the cabin. To
let them pick cotton alongside the other hired hands and
tenant farmers, to pay them for the work of two people
even though she was a sorry picker at first and Clay did
little work at all in his early years. On nights in the cabin's
bed with Clay asleep against her body, Bess imagined argu-
ments between the Boltons, imagined them in such detail
that she herself could hardly believe Mr. Bolton would let
those people stay in their house, bleed them of milk and
meat and money. Bess's own father would never have let
squatters settle in one of his tenant houses, had in fact run
off families in worse shape than Bess's—if you could call

her and Clay a family.

She and Mrs. Bolton had only met the one time, when the woman had said, "Mr. Bolton means for you to have the cow," and then shut the door. Bess had turned and called Clay, who had squatted in the yard by a toy horse carved from wood, and told him they were going home.

*

When she woke, in the road, she knew God had spoken to her through Jesus Christ. In a dream, He had appeared before her in the road with a new wagon and a team of strong yellow oxen behind Him, not moving, and He had knelt and pushed back the hair from her eyes and lifted her chin in His fingers. She couldn't see His face for the sun was too bright, but she could look on his boots and did, fine chocolate leather stitched with gold thread and no dust to mar them. She heard him say, Walk, witness what man can do if I live in his heart.

She rose, brushing away sand from her cheek, shaking sand from her dress, and started toward Coffeeville.

*

She had walked for two hours talking softly to herself when she heard the wagon and stepped from the road into the grass to give way to its berth. The driver, a tall man dressed in a suit, tie and derby hat, whoaed the mules pulling it and touched the brim of the hat and looked at her with his head tilted. He glanced behind him in the wagon. Then he seemed to arrive at a kind of peace and smiled, said she looked give out, asked her would she like a ride to town. She thanked him and climbed in the back amid children, who frowned at one another at her presence, the haze of flies she'd grown used to. A young one asked was she going to the doctor.

"No," she said, "to church."

She slept despite the wagon's bumpy ride and woke only when one of the children wiggled her toe.

"We here," the child said.

Her neck felt better, but still she moved it cautiously when she turned toward the Coffeeville Methodist Church, a simple sturdy building painted white and with a row of tall windows along its side, the glasses raised, people sitting in them, their backs to the world, attention focused inside. In front of the building, buggies, horses and mules stood shaded by pecan branches. Women in hats were unrolling blankets on the brown grass that sloped down to the graveyard, itself shaded by magnolias. From out of the windows she heard singing:

> Are you weak and heavy laden?
> Cumbered with a load of care?
> Precious Savior still our refuge,
> Take it to the Lord in prayer.

The children parted around her and spilled from the wagon, as if glad to be freed of her. The man stood and set the brake, then climbed down. He had a cloth-covered dish in his hand. "Here we are," he said, and put down his plate which she could smell—chicken, fried—and offered his hand. She took it, warm in hers, and the earth felt firm beneath her feet.

Tipping his hat, taking up the plate, he began to make his way through the maze of wagons and buggies and up the steps and inside. She stood waiting. The song ended and another began and more women—too busy to see her—hurried out a side door carrying cakes, and several children ran laughing down the hill, some rolling in the grass, and from somewhere a dog barked.

Two familiar men stepped out the front door, both dressed in dark suits and string ties. They began rolling cigarettes. When the young one noticed her he pointed with a match in his hand and the other looked and saw her too. They glanced at each other and began to talk, then Glaine Bolton hurried back inside. Marcus Eady stayed, watching her. His long gray hair swept back beneath his hat, his goatee combed to a point and his cheeks shaved clean. He lit his cigarette. Trailing a hand along the wood of the wall, he moved slowly down the steps and off the side of the porch and along the building beneath the windows, over the dirt toward a line of horses tied to a rail, the stock of a rifle outlined against the white paint of the building. When he got to the horse he began to stroke its mane and speak softly to it, all the while watching her.

The front door opened and the man who stepped out putting on his hat was Sheriff Waite, wearing a white shirt and thin black suspenders. He stood on the porch with his hands on his hips. She was holding onto the side of the wagon to keep from falling, and for a moment Waite seemed to stand beside his own twin, and then they blurred and she blinked them back into a single sheriff.

He had seen her. He glanced at Marcus Eady and patted the air with his hand to stay the man as he, Waite, came down the steps and through the wagons and buggies and horses and mules, laying his hands across the necks and rumps of the skittish animals nearest her to calm them. When he stood over her, bent as she was, she came only to his badge, which he wore pinned neatly to his shirt, stained beneath the arms with sweat. If he had a coat he'd removed it in the heat.

"Missus Freemont," he said. "What are you doing?"

"My boy needs burying," she said. "The Lord led me here."

For a moment, as he watched her, Waite held a look in his eyes that doubted that such a lord existed. What did he see in her face that made his own face both dreadful and aggrieved? What a sight she must be, bloodied, rank, listing up from the camp of the dead to here, the sunlit world of the living, framed in God's view from the sky in startling white cotton. She clung to the wagon's sideboard and felt her heart beat against it. More people had come onto the porch in their black and white clothes and were watching, stepping down into the churchyard. A woman put her hand over her mouth. Another hid a child's face. Marcus Eady had drawn his rifle and levered a round into its chamber. Glaine Bolton emerged from the church, moving people aside, and pointed toward Bess and Waite, who had reached to steady her. The man last out was the preacher, Travis Bolton. He held his Bible above his eyes to shade them so he might see. Then he pushed down the arm of his son trying to hold him back and left the boy frowning and came through the people, toward her.

SMASH AND GRAB
Michael Knight

At the last house on the left, the one with no security system signs staked on the lawn, no dog in the backyard, Cashdollar elbowed out a pane of glass in the kitchen door and reached through to unlock it from the inside. Though he was ninety-nine percent certain that the house was empty—he'd watched the owners leave himself—he paused a moment just across the threshold, listened carefully, heard nothing.

Satisfied, he padded through an archway into the dining room where he found a chest of silverware and emptied its contents into the pillowcase he'd brought. He was headed down the hall, looking for the master bedroom, hoping that, in the rush to make some New Year's Eve soiree, the lady of the house had left her jewelry in plain sight, when he saw a flash of white and his head was snapped back on his neck, the bones in his face suddenly aflame. He wobbled, dropped to his knees. Then a girlish grunt and another burst of pain and all he knew was darkness.

He came to with his wrists and ankles bound with duct tape to the arms and legs of a ladderback chair. His cheeks throbbed. His nose felt huge with ache. Opposite him, in an identical chair, a teenage girl was blowing lightly on the fingers of her left hand. There was a porcelain toilet tank lid, flecked with blood, across her lap. On it was arrayed a pair of cuticle scissors, a bottle of clear polish, cotton balls and a nail file. The girl glanced up at him now and he would have sworn she was pleased to find him awake.

"How's your face?" she said.

She was long-limbed, lean but not skinny, wearing a sweatshirt with the words SAINT BRIDGET'S VOLLEYBALL across the front in pastel plaids. Her hair was pulled into pigtails. She had on flannel boxers and pink wool socks. "It hurts like hell." His nostrils were plugged with blood, his voice buzzing like bad wiring in his head.

The girl did a sympathetic wince.

"I didn't think anyone was home," he said.

"I guess you cased the house?" she said. "Is that the word—cased?" Cashdollar nodded and she gave him a look, like she was sorry for spoiling his plans.

"I'm at boarding school. I just flew in this afternoon."

"I didn't see a light," he said.

"I was in the bathroom." She waggled her fingers at him. "I was on my left pinky when I heard the window break."

"Have you called the police?"

"Right after I knocked you out. You scared me so bad I practically just shouted my address into the phone and hung up." She giggled a little at herself. "I was afraid you'd wake up and kill me. That's why the tape. I'll call again if they aren't here soon." This last she delivered as if she regretted having to make him wait.

Cashdollar estimated at least ten minutes for the girl to drag him down the hall and truss him up, which meant that the police would be arriving momentarily. He had robbed houses in eleven states, had surprised his share of homeowners, but he'd never once had a run-in with the law. He was too fast on his feet for that, strictly smash and grab, never got greedy, never resorted to violence. Neither, however, had he ever been bashed unconscious with a toilet lid and duct-taped to a chair by a teenage girl.

"This boarding school," he said, "they don't send you home for Christmas?"

"I do Christmas with my mom," she said.

Cashdollar waited a moment for her to elaborate but she was quiet and he wondered if he hadn't hit on the beginnings of an angle here, wondered if he had time enough to work it. When it was clear that she wasn't going to continue, he prompted her. "Divorce is hard," he said.

The girl shrugged. "Everybody's divorced."

"So the woman I saw before—" He let the words trail off into a question.

"My father's girlfriend," she said. "One of." She rolled her eyes. Her eyes were a curious, almost fluorescent shade of green. "My father is the last of the big-time swingers."

"Do you like her?" he said. "Is she nice?"

"I hardly know her. She's a nurse. Regina something. She works for him. I think it's tacky if you want to know the truth."

They were in the dining room, though Cashdollar hadn't bothered to take it in when he was loading up the silverware. He saw crown molding. He saw paintings on the walls, dogs and dead birds done in oils, expensive but without resale value.

This was a doctor's house, he thought. It made him angry that he'd misread the presence of the woman, angrier even than the fact that he'd let himself get caught. He was thirty-six years old. That seemed to him just then like a long time to be alive.

"I'm surprised you don't have a date tonight," he said. "Pretty girl like you home alone on New Year's Eve."

He had his doubts about flattery—the girl seemed too sharp for that—but she took his remark in stride.

"Like I said, I just got in today and I'm away at school most of the year. Plus, I spend more time with my mother in California than my father so I don't really know anybody in Mobile."

"What's your name?" he said.

The girl hesitated. "I'm not sure I should tell you that."

"I just figured if you told me your name and I told you mine then you'd know somebody here."

"I don't think so," she said.

Cashdollar closed his eyes. He was glad that he wasn't wearing some kind of burglar costume, the black sweatsuit, the ski mask. He felt less obvious in street clothes. Tonight, he'd chosen a hunter green car coat, a navy turtleneck, khaki pants and boat shoes. He didn't bother wearing gloves. He wasn't so scary-looking this way, he thought, and when he asked the question that was on his mind, it might seem like one regular person asking a favor of another.

"Listen, I'm just going to come right out and say this, OK. I'm wondering what are the chances you'd consider letting me go?" The girl opened her mouth but Cashdollar went on before she could refuse and she settled back into her chair to let him finish.

"Because the police will be here soon and I don't want

to go to prison and I promise, if you let me, I'll leave the way I came in and vanish from your life forever."

The girl was quiet for a moment, her face patient and composed, as if waiting to be sure he'd said his piece. He could hear the refrigerator humming in the kitchen. A moth plinked against the chandelier over their heads. He wondered if it hadn't slipped in through the broken pane. The girl capped the bottle of nail polish, lifted the toilet lid from her lap without disturbing the contents and set it on the floor beside her chair.

"I'm sorry," she said. "I really am but you did break into the house and you put my father's silverware in your pillowcase and I'm sure you would have taken other things if I hadn't hit you on the head. If you want, I'll tell the police that you've been very nice, but I don't think it's right for me to let you go."

In spite of—or because of—her genial demeanor, Cashdollar was beginning to feel like his heart was on the blink; it felt as thick and rubbery as a hot water bottle in his chest. He held his breath and strained against his bonds, hard enough to hop his chair, once, twice, but the tape held fast. He sat there, panting.

The girl said, "Let me ask you something. Let's say I was asleep or watching TV or whatever and I didn't hear the window break. Let's say you saw me first— what would you have done?"

He didn't have to think about his reply. "I would have turned around and left the house. I've never hurt anyone in my whole life." The girl stared at him for a long moment then dropped her eyes and fanned her fingers, studied her nails. She didn't look altogether pleased. To the backs of her hands, she said, "I believe you."

As if to punctuate her sentence, the doorbell chimed, followed by four sharp knocks, announcing the arrival of the police.

*

While he waited, Cashdollar thought about prison. The possibility of incarceration loomed forever on the periphery of his life but he'd never allowed himself to waste a lot of time considering the specifics. He told himself that at least he wasn't leaving anyone behind, wasn't ruining anyone else's life, though even as he filled his head with reassurances, he understood that they were false and his pulse was roaring in his ears, his lungs constricting. He remembered this one break-in over in Pensacola when some sound he made—a rusty hinge, a creaking floorboard— startled the owner of the house from sleep. The bedroom was dark and the man couldn't see Cashdollar standing at the door. "Joyce?" he said.

"Is that you, Joyce?" There was such sadness, such longing in his voice that Cashdollar knew Joyce was never coming back. He pitied the man, of course, but at the same time, he felt as if he was watching him through a window, felt outside the world looking in rather than in the middle of things with the world pressing down around him. The man rolled over, mumbled his way back to sleep, and Cashdollar crept out of the house feeling sorry for himself. He hadn't thought about that man in years. Now, he could hear voices in the next room but he couldn't make out what they were saying. It struck him that they were taking too long and he wondered if this wasn't what people meant when they described time bogging down at desperate moments.

The girl rounded the corner into the dining room trailing a pair of uniformed police officers, the first a white guy, straight out of central casting, big and pudgy, his tunic crumpled into his slacks, his belt slung low under his belly, the second, a black woman, small with broad shoulders, her hair twisted into braids under her cap. "My friend—" The girl paused, shot a significant look at Cashdollar. "—Patrick, surprised him in the dining room and the burglar hit him with the toilet thingy and taped him up. Patrick, these are Officers Hildebran and Pruitt." She tipped her head right, then left to indicate the man and the woman respectively.

Officer Pruitt circled around behind Cashdollar's chair.

"What was the burglar doing with a toilet lid?"

"That's a mystery," the girl said.

"Why haven't you cut him loose?"

"We didn't know what to do for sure," the girl said. "He didn't seem to be hurt too bad and we didn't want to disturb the crime scene. On TV, they always make a big deal out of leaving everything just so."

"I see," said Officer Pruitt, exactly as if she didn't see at all. "And you did your nails to pass the time?" She pointed at the manicure paraphernalia.

The girl made a goofy, self-deprecating face, all eyebrows and lips, twirled her finger in the air beside her ear. Officer Hildebran wandered over to the window. Without facing the room, he said, "I'll be completely honest with you, Miss Schnell—" "Daphne," the girl said and Cashdollar had the sense that her interjection was meant for him.

Officer Hildebran turned, smiled. "I'll be honest, Daphne, we sometimes recover some of the stolen property but—"

"He didn't take anything," the girl said.

Officer Hildebran raised his eyebrows. "No?"

"He must have panicked," Daphne said.

Cashdollar wondered what had become of his pillow-case, figured it was still in the hall where the girl had ambushed him, hoped the police didn't decide to poke around back there. Officer Pruitt crouched at his knees to take a closer look at the duct tape.

"You all right?" she said.

He nodded, cleared his throat.

"Where'd the tape come from?"

"I don't know," he said. "I was out cold."

"Regardless," Officer Hildebran was saying to Daphne, "unless there's a reliable eyewitness—"

Officer Pruitt sighed. "There is an eyewitness." She raised her eyes, regarded Cashdollar's battered face.

"Oh," Officer Hildebran said. "Right. You think you could pick him out of a line-up?"

"It all happened pretty fast," Cashdollar said.

And so it went, as strange and vivid as a fever dream, their questions, his answers, their questions, Daphne's an-swers—he supposed that she was not the kind of girl likely to arouse suspicion, not the kind of girl people were in-clined to disbelieve—until Officers Hildebran and Pruitt were satisfied, more or less. They seemed placated by the fact that his injuries weren't severe and that nothing had actually been stolen. Officer Pruitt cut the tape with a utility knife and Cashdollar walked them to the door like he was welcome in this house. He invented contact infor-mation, assured them that he'd be down in the morning to look at mugshots. He didn't know what had changed

Daphne's mind and, watching the police make their way down the sidewalk and out of his life, he didn't care. He shut the door and said, "Is Daphne your real name?" He was just turning to face her when she clubbed him with the toilet lid again.

*

Once more, he woke in the ladderback chair, wrists and ankles bound, but this time Daphne was seated cross-legged on the floor, leaned back, her weight on her hands. He saw her as if through a haze, as if looking through a smudgy lens, noticed her long neck, the smooth skin on the insides of her thighs. "Yes," Daphne said.

"What?"

"Yes, my name is Daphne."

"Oh," he said.

His skull felt full of sand.

"I'm sorry for conking you again," she said. "I don't know what happened. I mean, it was such a snap decision to lie to the police and then that woman cut the tape and I realized I don't know the first thing about you and I freaked." She paused. "What's your name?" she said.

Cashdollar felt as if he was being lowered back into himself from a great height, gradually remembering how it was to live in his body. Before he was fully aware of what he was saying, he'd given her an honest answer. "Leonard," he said.

Daphne laughed. "I wasn't expecting that," she said. "I didn't think anybody named anybody Leonard anymore."

"I'm much older than you."

"You're not so old. What are you, forty?"

"Thirty-six."

Daphne said, "Oops."

"I think I have a concussion," Cashdollar said.

Daphne wrinkled her nose apologetically and pushed to her feet and brushed her hands together. "Be right back," she said. She ducked into the kitchen, returned with a highball glass which she held under his chin. He smelled scotch, let her bring it to his mouth. It tasted expensive.

"Better?" Daphne said.

Cashdollar didn't answer. He'd been inclined to feel grateful but hadn't the vaguest idea where this was going now. She sat on the floor and he watched her sip from the glass. She made a retching face, shuddered, regrouped. "At school one time, I drank two entire bottles of Robitussin cough syrup. I hallucinated that my Klimt poster was coming to life. It was very sexual. My roommate called the paramedics."

"Is that right?" Cashdollar said.

"My father was in Aruba when it happened," she said. "He was with an AMA rep named Farina Hoyle. I mean, what kind of a name is Farina Hoyle? He left her there and flew all the way back to make sure I was all right."

"That's nice, I guess," Cashdollar said.

Daphne nodded and smiled, half-sly, half-something else. Cashdollar couldn't put his finger on what he was seeing in her face. "It isn't true," she said. "The Robitussin's true. Farina Hoyle's true. Aruba's true."

"What are you going to do with me?" Cashdollar said.

Daphne peered into the glass.

"I don't know," she said.

They were quiet for a minute. Daphne swirled the whisky. Cashdollar's back itched and he rubbed it on the chair. When Daphne saw what he was doing, she moved behind the chair to scratch it for him and he tipped forward to give her better access. Her touch raised goosebumps, made his skin jump like horseflesh.

"Are you married?" she said.

He told her, "No."

"Divorced?"

He shook his head. Her hand went still between his shoulder blades. He heard her teeth click on the glass.

"You poor thing," she said. "Haven't you ever been in love?"

"I think you should cut me loose," Cashdollar said. Daphne came around the chair and sat on his knee, draped her arm over his shoulder.

"How often do you do this? Rob houses, I mean."

"I do it when I need the money," he said.

"When was the last time?" Her face was close enough that he could smell the liquor on her breath.

"A while ago," he said. "Could I have another sip of that?" She helped him with the glass. He felt the scotch behind his eyes. The truth was he'd done an apartment house just last week, waited at the door for somebody to buzz him up, then broke the locks on the places where no one was home. He was in and out in less than an hour. Just now, however, he didn't see the percentage in the truth. He said, "I only ever do rich people and I give half my take to Jerry's Kids."

Daphne socked him in the chest.

"Ha, ha," she said.

"Isn't that what you want to hear?" he said. "Right? You're looking for a reason to let me go?"

"I don't know," she said.

He shrugged. "Who's to say it isn't true?"

"Jerry's Kids," she said.

She was smiling and he smiled back. He couldn't help liking this girl. He liked that she was smart and that she wasn't too afraid of him. He liked that she had the guts to bullshit the police.

"Ha, ha," he said.

Daphne knocked back the last of the scotch, then skated her socks over the hardwood floor, headed for the bay window.

"Do you have a car?" she said, parting the curtains. "I don't see a car."

"I'm around the block," he said.

"What do you drive?"

"Honda Civic."

Daphne raised her eyebrows.

"It's inconspicuous," he said.

She skated back over to his chair and slipped her hand into his pocket and rooted for his keys. Cashdollar flinched. There were only two keys on the ring, his car and his apartment. For some reason, this embarrassed him. "It really is a Honda," Daphne said.

*

There was a grandfather clock in the corner but it had died at half past eight who knew how long ago and his watch was out of sight beneath the duct tape and Cashdollar was beginning to worry about the time. He guessed Daphne had been gone for twenty minutes, figured he was safe until after midnight, figured her father and his lady friend would at least ring in the New Year before calling it a night. He put the hour around 11 but he couldn't be sure and for all he knew, Daphne was out there joyriding in his car and you couldn't tell what might happen at a party on New Year's Eve. Somebody might get angry. Somebody might have too much to drink. Somebody might be so crushed with love they can't wait another minute to get home. He went on thinking like this until he heard what sounded like a garage door rumbling open and his mind went blank and every ounce of his perception funneled down into his ears. For a minute, he heard nothing—he wasn't going to mistake silence for safety a second time—then a door opened in the kitchen and Daphne breezed into the room. "Took me a while to find your car," she said. She had changed clothes. Now she was wearing an electric-blue parka with fur inside the hood and white leggings and knee-high alpine boots. "What time is it?" he said.

But she passed through without stopping, disappeared into the next room.

"You need to let me go," he said.

When she reappeared, she was carrying a stereo speaker. He watched her go into the kitchen. She returned a minute later without the speaker, took the parka off and draped it on a chair.

"It's a good thing you've got a hatchback," Daphne said.

For the next half hour, she shuttled between the house and the garage, bearing valuables each trip, first the rest of the stereo, then the TV and the VCR, then his pillowcase of silverware, then an armload of expensive-looking suits and on and on until Cashdollar was certain that his car would hold no more. Still she kept it up. Barbells, golf clubs, a calfskin luggage set. A pair of antique pistols. A dusty classical guitar. A baseball signed by someone dead and famous. With each passing minute, Cashdollar could feel his stomach tightening and it was all he could do to keep his mouth shut but he had the sense that he should leave her be, that this didn't have anything to do with him. He pictured his little Honda bulging with the accumulated property of another man's life, flashed to his apartment in his mind, unmade bed, lawn chairs in the living room, coffee mug in the sink. He made a point of never holding on to anything anybody else might want to steal. There was not a single thing in his apartment that it would hurt to lose, nothing he couldn't live without. Daphne swung back into the room, looking frazzled. She huffed at a wisp of stray hair that had fallen across her eyes.

"There," she said.

Cashdollar said, "You're crazy."

Daphne dismissed him with a wave.

"You're out of touch," she said. "I'm your average sophomore."

"What'll you tell the cops?"

"I like Stockholm Syndrome but I think they're more likely to believe you made me lie under threat of death." She lifted the hem of her sweatshirt to wipe her face, exposing her belly, the curve of her ribs, pressed it first against her right eye, then her left as if dabbing tears.

"Ha, ha," he said.

Daphne said, "I'll get the scissors."

She went out again, came back again. The tape fell away like something dead.

Cashdollar rubbed his wrists a second, pushed to his feet and they stood there looking at each other. Her eyes, he decided, were the color of a jade pendant he had stolen years ago. That pendant pawned for seven hundred dollars. It flicked through his mind that he should kiss her and that she would let him but he restrained himself. He had no business kissing teenage girls. Then, as if she could read his thoughts, Daphne slapped him across the face. Cashdollar palmed his cheek, blinked the sting away, watched her doing a girlish bob and weave, her thumbs tucked inside her fists.

"Let me have it," she said.

"Quit," he said.

"Wimp," she said. "I dropped you twice."

"I'm gone," he said.

Right then, she poked him in the nose. It wouldn't have hurt so much if she hadn't already hit him with the toilet lid but as it was, his eyes watered up, his vision filled with tiny sparkles. Without thinking, he balled his hand and punched her in the mouth, not too hard, a reflex, just enough to sit her down, but right away he felt sick at what he'd done. He held his palms out, like he was trying to stop traffic.

"I didn't mean that," he said. "That was an accident. I've never hit a girl. I've never hurt anyone in my whole life."

Daphne touched her bottom lip, smudging her fingertip with blood.

"This will break his heart," she said.

She smiled at Cashdollar and he could see blood in the spaces between her teeth. The sight of her dizzied him with sadness. He thought how closely linked were love and pain. Daphne extended a hand, limp-wristed, ladylike. Her nails were perfect.

"Now tape me to the chair," she said.

FLEET'S EATS:
TALES OF THE CULINARY UNDERGROUND
John T. Edge

"I met my idol on the first day of grade school," Norfleet Reichle tells me between pulls on a menthol-flavored Doral. "Willie D. Thompson was his name. I walked in the bathroom and there he was, standing on the toilet seat, taking a dump. Momma said I had wings 'til right about then."

It's five-thirty on a blustery Monday morning in January of this year. Norfleet, a stolid fifty-two-year-old with a wide and welcoming face and a half-cocked smile, is holding court from a tattered recliner. Attired in khaki shorts and a v-neck t-shirt, he wears neither socks nor shoes. Since about three-thirty, Norfleet has been peeling potatoes and shucking corn. I had planned to document his day from start to finish, but I couldn't wrench my bones from bed at four, when Norfleet usually rises. So I'm playing catch-up and gulping coffee in an attempt to clear my head. Norfleet, on the other hand, is at full gallop.

He heaves from his perch and heads for the narrow kitchen at the north end of the house he shares with his wife, Sheila. "Did I tell you about how I jumped 92 feet into 22 feet of water?" Norfleet is way ahead of me. "Now, don't get me wrong," he says, pulling the top from a tub of marshmallow fluff and fixing me with a gaze devoid of even a trace of irony, "I like to take a drink of whiskey. But I wasn't drunk; I was just drinking."

*

Norfleet Reichle likes to drink. He also likes to cook. For the last two years, he's done more cooking than drinking. His wife is pleased. So are his regulars, the dirt farmers, fish farmers, doctors, and lawyers of Columbus, Mississippi, who stop by his house every weekday for lunch. Though his address is listed on state tax rolls as a bed and breakfast, and a cypress placard by the front door reads FLEET'S EATS, the ranch-style home in which Norfleet and Sheila live is best understood as a sort of liminal restaurant on the cusp of legitimacy, the kind of place where the laundry room serves as a staging area for iced tea service and the carport does double duty as a pantry.

The concept is not unique. Annie Keith's, a meat-'n'-three in Atlanta, Georgia, began its path to legal status in the kitchen of a brick midtown bungalow. Good Ole Home Cooking in McCormick, South Carolina, started serving midday meals to local laborers from a doublewide garage. Customers at Colonel Hawk's in Bardstown, Kentucky, once announced their arrival by driving around back of the proprietor's home and clanging a bell. Without exception, these proto-restaurants are remembered fondly for their food, if not their stubborn homeliness and lack of pretense.

Perhaps it's the South's tradition of privation-fueled enterprise—a similar legacy spurred the rise of Cuban

home restaurants known as *paladares*—but the informal
economy of what are sometimes known as backdoor
restaurants remains strong. Besides Fleet's Eats, I know of
five other spots in Mississippi. Some, like Peggy's in
Philadelphia—which still serves lunch from a makeshift
plank buffet spanning the hallway of the Webb family
home—have made the leap to legitimacy. Others, like a
house restaurant in the capitol of Jackson, operate thanks
to a wink-and-nod arrangement that draws local glitterati
to their stoop but, in the interest of keeping the health department functionaries at bay, forbids regulars from
divulging the name and address of the kind lady who
dishes up what may be the city's best fried chicken and
sweet potato pie.

*

"If you're cooking two meats and five vegetables,
sometimes you got to call the big dogs in," says Norfleet,
as he muscles tubs of vegetables from the refrigerator to
the Radar Range to what passes for his steam trolley, a
folding table topped with eight daisy-ringed Crock Pots
and a ginger jar lamp. Purple hull peas go in one crock;
fresh corn in another; mashed potatoes, cut with a block
of preternaturally yellow oleo, in a third.

It's now about eight in the morning. Sheila (a doe-
eyed paralegal from the Delta who fell hard for Norfleet's
schoolboy-gone-to-seed charm) has been up since six-
thirty, slicing bananas for pudding and mixing cornmeal
batter for muffins. Between muffin batches, she works the
phone, faxing menus to the likes of Highway 82 Pawn and
First Baptist Church of Columbus, and taking calls for
menu recitations from regulars. "Frank, you better come

out here today," she chirps. "I got a butterflied pork chop with lots of fat on it, and it's got your name all over it."

When Norfleet takes another cigarette break, I turn my attention from scribbling notes to taking inventory of my surroundings. What was once a sun porch is now over-taken by a ten-seat table and case after case of Fleet's homemade pepper vinegar, pea relish, and spicy vegetable juice. The dining room now boasts seating for ten. To ac-commodate four-seat and six-seat tables, the couch in the family room has been shoved against the back wall, be-tween the recliner and the television.

*

Norfleet Reichle did not aim to be a restaurateur. Upon graduation from high school, he pursued Jef-ferson's agrarian ideal by way of farming the rich prairie that stretches eastward from Columbus through the black belt of Alabama. Norfleet worked the land for more than twenty-five years, raising hogs and cattle, soybeans and winter wheat. At one point he rented and cropped thir-teen hundred acres. Two straight summers of too much rain, however, brought his farming career to a shuddering halt. In 1993, along with his first wife, Norfleet took over a plate lunch place on the outskirts of Columbus. "I didn't know a thing about running a restaurant," says Norfleet, "but I knew everything I needed to know about cooking." But when Norfleet lost his first wife, he lost his first restau-rant. Another restaurant followed. It didn't take either. Fleet's Eats wasn't hatched as a third try. It evolved out of a catering and lunch delivery business that Norfleet and Sheila began with the hope that they would pick up a few extra dollars until something better came along.

These days, though the personal lives of Norfleet and Sheila appear to be in retreat, the house is not wholly absent the trappings of a typical working-class home: Duck prints and cross-stitched homilies bedeck the formal living room; a bookshelf stacked with family portraits, *World Book Encyclopedias*, and John Grisham novels stands tall alongside the fireplace; and pillows, appliquéd with doleful angels, dot a plaid couch in the family room.

Amazingly enough, the kitchen may well be the public room least affected by Norfleet and Sheila's stab at homegrown commerce. The Reichles use little specialized equipment. No Buffalo chopper, no Hobart mixer. In fact, if you arrive after Sheila has put away the two electric skillets in which she fries the chicken and pork chops, and you squint your eyes just a bit, you might believe that the oversized platter of deviled eggs on the counter is intended for a 100-year-flood family reunion instead of the midday crush of regulars at a renegade restaurant.

*

The midday meal comes early in Columbus. If, like many of the customers at Fleet's Eats, you begin your day at first light, then a ten-forty-five trencherman's lunch is the perfect answer to a five-thirty biscuit-and-coffee breakfast. As nine begets ten, prep work slows. By ten, Norfleet is standing on ready. Ditto Sheila. All eight of the Crock Pots are full. The wall oven is stuffed with trays of fried pork chops. A napkin-wrapped basket of brown-and-serve rolls sits on the counter alongside a Tupperware tub of cucumber and onion salad. And row upon row of plastic-wrapped slices of apple pie—a result of Sheila's recent and intensive study of *Betty Crocker's Cookbook*—await the crowds to come.

Since sometime around daybreak, Norfleet has quit the recliner in favor of taking his cigarette breaks while leaning at the kitchen sink, flicking ashes down the drain. That's where he is when the first customer walks through the back door, tracing a path alongside the bright orange extension cord that snakes from a carport plug to the kitchen counter. Norfleet has yet to serve a meal, but, as he surveys what he has wrought, he pulls on a Doral with a sort of post-coital bliss, as if, seven hours into his workday, it's all gravy from here.

For the next couple of hours, Sheila pours tea and makes change from what was once the silver drawer, while Norfleet monitors Crock Pot levels. Though he does not shirk his duties, it's Sheila who shoulders the brunt of service. Norfleet is busy working the crowd, calling most everyone by name. Between tales of how he cooked a loggerhead turtle gumbo and what inspired him to strip the meat from catfish frames to make croquettes dubbed "cat puppies," he steals glances at the Weather Channel, justifying interest in cable television by pronouncing, "Anybody with any damn sense is interested in the weather."

*

He rides the crest of the lunch rush for a good hour and a half. But by one in the afternoon, Norfleet is out of red beans and rice, his back is cramping, and he is mortal once again. Before the day is over, he and Sheila will serve forty-five, maybe fifty lunches. If they're lucky—and if Norfleet doesn't lose a double-or-nothing wager to a table of farmers in the mood to gamble for a free lunch—they might net $150. It's barely a living wage, but that doesn't trouble Norfleet. "I'm not in it for the money," he tells me as he scrapes a plate. "I like people, I like cooking, and I gotta pay my bills, so I figured I might as well give this a try."

As he works his way through a stack of dirty dishes, the sink begins to empty, and, by my measure, Norfleet grows restless. Without the prospect of work to occupy his head and hands, his country-fried ebullience fades. I'm expecting a breakdown, some sort of epiphanic moment wherein Norfleet pledges to chuck it all for a job as an oil-rig cook.

But I've been reading his mood all wrong. When I slip on my coat and begin to say my goodbyes, he sidles up to me, intent upon talking about his plans for the future, about how he's going to add seating for fifty patrons and convert the carport into a true restaurant kitchen. Norfleet proves to be a compelling door-talker. When I try again to take my leave he asks, *sotto voce*, what I think about the prospect of making sardines by pickling catfish fingerlings. What I read as panic and pathos was actually the birth of a notion. "I'm thinking that I wouldn't have to skin the little fellas," he tells me, "but I would have to clip off the fins, and I might have to gut 'em."

DOWN THE SHORE EVERYTHING'S ALL RIGHT
Michelle Richmond

We're driving through the Lincoln Tunnel en route to
Jersey when Ivan turns off the tape player and puts his
hand on my thigh. I know what this means. It means he's
gearing up to tell me the story. He'll be telling it in a way
that suggests he has never told me this story before, that
he has never told it to anyone, that it's coming straight to
me from his heart, where he has saved it all these years.
Each time the story is a little different; he adds or subtracts
a few details, spruces up the dialogue, increases or de-
creases the temperature of that March day in northern
California by a couple of degrees. Each time he tells the
story, he has a new hook, an improved first line. This
whole day has been planned in homage to that story, the
story of the greatest moment of his life. We've rented a car
and are on our way to Asbury Park.

It occurs to me that this is the day I'm going to break
up with him, that there is no more putting it off. After four
years, it seems fitting that we should end our relationship
in Asbury Park on the occasion of his second pilgrimage,
and it seems somehow more civil than if I were to break

the news to him anywhere else—over dessert at Edgar's, say, or in our bed on West 85th.

Ivan first traveled to Asbury Park in 1982, soon after the release of *Nebraska,* three years after supposedly meeting Bruce Springsteen on a service road in San Mateo, California. He had gone to the Jersey Shore with his brother, driven cross-country from San Francisco hoping to get a glimpse of the world beyond the West Coast, and, more important, the world of Bruce. At the time, I was fourteen years old and a big fan of Madonna, and the crowd I ran with thought of Bruce as some overly patriotic guy with a redneck heart and sweaty bandanna. Bruce was a Jersey thing; being from the Gulf Coast, we didn't get it.

"There's this booth right on the boardwalk," Ivan says, fumbling with the hem of my skirt. "Madame Marie. I hope she's still there. Madame Marie read my palm, you know. She said I'd meet a girl with ringlets in her hair."

"Did you?"

"Not that I recall. But I did have this girlfriend named Sandy Cho who went to a Halloween party as Shirley Temple."

We exit the tunnel amid a cloud of exhaust fumes. An Atlantic City–bound bus screeches and sighs in front of us. This morning, Sam Champion on Channel Seven promised light showers in the city, heavy wind and rain on the Jersey Shore.

"I've gotta show you the Stone Pony. That's where Bruce met the band—Gary W. Tallent, Danny Federici, The Big Man, Vini Mad Dog Lopez, Miami Steve Van Zant. And we've got to see the tunnel of love, of course. Remember that song?" He sings it for me. "*Fat man sitting on* *a little stool, takes the money from my hand while his eyes take a walk all over you...*Did I ever tell you I got a picture of him?"

"You might have mentioned it."

"Too bad about the film."

When I first met Ivan, I thought the Bruce bit was a fish story he'd eventually let go of, a sort of introductory hoorah intended to impress me, like those guys who woo you with expensive restaurants only to settle into pizza-by-the-slice and Chinese-in-a-box as soon as they have your attention. I was a college girl from Alabama, visiting New York City for the first time. Ivan bought me dirty martinis at a place called Sabrina's, and we talked until the lights went down and a waitress in blue tights asked us to leave. Ivan also had stories about going to a Kings game with Tom Hanks and meeting Huey Lewis at a party, stories that came up only once, off-handedly, never to be repeated. But he has held tightly to his story about Bruce and the camera with no film, never budging, recounting it once or twice a year for various audiences, as if by sheer pig-head-edness and repetition he might make it true.

He rolls down the window and the smell of New Jersey invades the car, industrial and sad and vaguely mean-spirited, a lingering fog of factory smoke and hair spray. Everything looks dismal from the passenger seat, where I am silently rehearsing my break-up speech.

"I'm exiting the drive-through at McDonald's," Ivan begins.

"I thought you said it was Taco Bell," I say, testing him, hoping to catch him in a lie.

"No, definitely McDonald's. I've got a Big Mac in my lap, a large Coke propped between my knees. There's this Mustang stopped in front of me. Another car has pulled in alongside him, and they're talking, blocking the intersection. I honk and the guy in the Mustang waves a hand out the window, like an apology, says goodbye to his friend, and pulls out. And I'm thinking, wow, I know that voice. That 'Bye, now,' I've heard it before. Bruce said it when he exited the stage in Oakland. But I'm a seventeen-year-old kid, right? And this guy's my idol, and I don't believe for a second it could be true."

"I once met Elizabeth Montgomery when I was waiting tables in Tuscaloosa," I say, but Ivan's so caught up in the miracle of the remembered moment that he doesn't hear me, or at least my words don't register.

It doesn't take long for the Turnpike to become less appalling. Smokestacks slowly disappear, giving way to heavily wooded roadsides and expansive medians, the first green I've seen in months. Pale, immaculate roofs peek over the tops of ugly sound barriers, and I think of the people in those regular houses, living regular lives, the kind I felt destined for until Ivan persuaded me to abandon wide Southern beaches for big-city sidewalks. Half of my motive for breaking up with him is that I blame him for bringing me to New York City, where living quarters are miniscule and people are unkind. The other half is that I'm tired of his stories. Not just Bruce, but the others. Like the time he was walking down the street and saw a group of workmen handling a huge plate-glass window several stories above, and in the next instant the glass was suddenly in freefall, shattering inches behind him.

"A split-second difference in my pace," he once told me, "a moment of hesitation as I walked, and the window would have taken off my head." It seems to me the stuff of fantasy, his frequent meetings with celebrities and his hair-breadth escapes from death. Ivan lives in a dramatic world of his own making, in which he is a magnet for the incredible and the impossible, simultaneously inviting the miraculous and the macabre. The bottom line is this: I do not believe him. In the beginning his stories charmed me. Now, they only annoy me. I want him to be honest, dependable, perhaps a little mundane. I want to be the one person to whom he feels compelled to tell the truth. And there is the lingering fear that there are other, less innocent lies—lies relating to the weekend trips to Quebec with other teachers from his school, lies to explain the frequent and panicked voice of his ex-girlfriend on our answering machine.

"Once we're on the service road I pull up beside the Mustang, you know, just to check it out," Ivan continues. "There he is. It's Bruce. I'm not believing it. He's got Gary U.S. Bonds singing 'Rendezvous' on the tape deck. So I roll down my window and yell, 'Bruce,' and he looks over at me and gives me this wave. Real stupid, I shout, 'Welcome to San Mateo!' and he starts motioning for me to pull over. I do, and he does, and he gets out of the car, and then he's shaking my hand. I've got this point-and-snap in the glove compartment, and when I ask him if I can take a picture he says, 'Sure, why not.' If there had been film in the camera I'd have a picture of Bruce in a plaid flannel shirt and ripped jeans, just standing there looking slightly amused, with Togo's in the background. He's on his way to San Jose, but he says, 'Why don't you give me your phone number. I'll call you.' So I write it on the back of a crusty old road map, and then he pulls out, and I'm thinking, there's no way that just happened."

I finish the story for him, because I know the last line.

No matter how it starts, it always ends the same way. "Greatest moment of your life," I say.

"Not anymore. Second greatest moment of my life."

"What was the first?"

"Day I met you." He leans over and kisses me on the cheek, and I feel about this small, and I'm wondering how I'm going to pull off the break-up speech. And then I think maybe Asbury Park is all wrong, because it's a place he loves and if I break up with him there, maybe the place itself will be tainted. I should have thought of that before. I should have considered his theory of cross-contamination, how a thing can only be special in one kind of way. According to his theory, you don't take your new girlfriend to the same vacation spot you went with the old girlfriend, and you never fall in love with a woman who has the same first name as someone you loved before. It stands to reason, then, that he doesn't believe in making bad memories in a place where you've already made good ones.

"I have something to tell you," I say.

*

He cranks up the radio. "Out with it, bubba." That's what he calls me sometimes, bubba, because I'm from Alabama.

"I can't do this anymore."

"Do what?"

"This. Us."

He looks over at me, laughing. "Very funny. No, really. What did you want to tell me?"

"I'm serious."

He looks at me again. There's a tiny mole on the curve of his chin I never noticed before, not in four years of looking at him up close. "You're kidding me."

"It's just not working."

We pass a hitch-hiker in green corduroy pants. Her sign says she'll pay half the gas. "I spy me a hitch-hiker," I say, trying to lighten the moment with a game Ivan and I used to play every time we took a road trip. "I spy me a rabbit." The rule is that you can spy anything as long as it's animate, and the first one to repeat something loses.

"What do you want me to do?" Ivan says. "You want to move? You want to get married? We'll get married if that's it. We'll move out of the city. Get a place in Asbury Park, maybe, you'll like it there, it's real quiet in the winters. Or go down South. You want to go down South?"

"That won't solve it."

"Where's this coming from? What did I do?"

"You didn't do anything."

Silence, except for Howard Stern on the radio. He's interviewing a leading child psychologist, quizzing her on the size of her breasts. He wants to know if her breasts get in the way of her social work. She wants to know if his stupidity gets in the way of his career. She postulates that Howard Stern was breast-fed until the age of ten or so and thus his fascination with the mammary gland. She suggests that he wants to sleep with his mother. "Whoa-ho!" he says. "Easy, baby. I'll tell you who I want to sleep with. I want to sleep with *your* mother!" Howard's sidekick, Robin, tells him to behave.

"Maybe we should turn around," I say.

"We've come this far. We've got the car for the day. May as well."

A couple of minutes later we exit the turnpike, then drive in silence for a long time toward the shore. It begins to rain. The windshield wipers of our plastic rent-a-car keep sticking, and every couple of minutes I have to lean out the window and lift the wipers from the glass to get them moving again.

Our route takes us through broken-down towns that all look pretty much the same: old factories with soot-scarred windows, bent cars parked permanently in driveways, filthy little grocery stores with big white banners in the windows, advertising pork roast and Pampers. Ivan watches the slick road while I watch the odometer. It clicks off the miles with a slowness that reminds me of Alabama, Sunday drives with my parents and sisters through green empty places that inevitably ended at some abandoned length of railroad, the crossing signals long defunct. At one point Ivan reaches over and opens the glove compartment, then fumbles for a cassette. When he does this I move my knees aside, but the rental car is small and it's impossible not to touch. His hand brushing the back of my knee feels natural for about half a second, and then it's just embarrassing. He jerks it away, like I'm made of fiberglass or fire, and says, "See if you can find "Darkness on the Edge of Town."

As the opening song plays Ivan's hands beat the steering wheel, only vaguely in rhythm with the music. It's been about twenty miles since he looked my way. I know the story that goes with this song, how this was the first album he ever bought. How he took it home and put it on the turntable in the bedroom he shared with his brother at his family's new house in Burlingame, then listened to it for an entire day, the same song, hundreds of times.

Halfway through the song he pops the cassette out of the player. "How about the Stockholm tape?" he says. I fish through the glove compartment and find it. Bruce's version of "Jersey Girl," by Tom Waits, is playing as we pull into Asbury Park. *Now baby won't you come with me, cause down the shore everything's alright, you and your baby on a Saturday night. Nothing matters in this whole wide world when you're in love with a Jersey girl. Sing sha la la la la...* Like most of Bruce's own songs, "Jersey Girl" is two parts hope, one part working-man blues, and another part lusty despair.

A red Camaro passes on our left. The driver, a middle-aged woman with tattoos, gives us a happy wave, then guns the engine and moves on ahead of us. After Bruce, we hear Tom Waits doing the same song in his low-down rumble. When Tom Waits sings "Jersey Girl," you get the feeling that nothing is all right anywhere, and nowhere is less all right than where you are right now.

The rain is coming down hard, and the wind is pushing our two-door all over the road. The whole town looks deserted. You can tell from the crumbling facades of big, handsomely built hotels that wealthy people once vacationed here, then abandoned the place when it ceased to be fashionable. We park at a shut-down gas station across the street from the Tunnel of Love. The tunnel is nothing more than a hole carved into a low cement wall, the entrance decorated with a fading mural. I remember my second kiss ever—in the haunted house ride at Six Flags over Georgia. The guy's name was Jason Lowery. He put his hand up my shirt as our vehicle tipped toward a vast hall of floating skeletons. I felt a strange electricity on my skin, hundreds of tiny pin-pricks circling my nipple.

"There used to be a drive-in theater back there," Ivan says, pointing somewhere beyond the defunct amusement ride. "Did I ever tell you about the freeway drive-in?"

I shake my head no rather than answering aloud, just to force him to look at me. He doesn't.

"When I was in grammar school, my parents had this house above Daly City. From the window of our bedroom my brother and I could see the screen of the Geneva Drive-In across the freeway. Late at night, when we were supposed to be asleep, we'd lean out the window and watch the show. They played mostly sex flicks. We couldn't hear any sound, so we'd make up our own words. Blonde girls with enormous tanned breasts and plump red mouths saying things like, 'I think it's the carburetor' or 'Beam me up, Scotty.'"

I imagine him, age seven, with that bushy black hair I've seen in his old school photos. He's leaning out the window, his small face intersected by the shadows of a gigantic film, his features transformed frame by frame as naked bodies shift on the screen.

Rain is leaking through the passenger-side window onto my lap. Ivan takes off his windbreaker and arranges it over my legs. "You ever go to the drive-in?"

"We didn't have one in Mobile. If you wanted to see a movie you had to go to Springdale Mall."

*

We talk about movies for a while, and then about what they call the New South, how it's short on character and big on strip malls. I recount for him the steeple wars waged by the Southern Baptist churches of my childhood, how my parents emptied their pockets each week to contribute to the war chest of Bay Street Baptist Church, how the new steeple towered over Mobile Bay, white and gleaming like a sword.

Then we talk about a weekend we once spent at the Russian River, when Ivan got sick from Swedish pancakes at the River Inn. "Remember swimming out to the sand bar?" Ivan asks. For a moment we are both lost in the sweet-smelling warmth of the river, the memory of it running narrow and swift behind the inn. That night we hauled cold beer to the sand bar in a small Styrofoam chest, then lay on our backs and watched cars pass on the highway that hugged the high banks of the river. It's strange how a relationship can go on living for hours after you both know it's dead, how we can sit here and talk about nothing as if everything's the same, as if there are no decisions to be made.

When the rain lets up, Ivan starts the car again and we drive about a mile down the shore. We park in front of a boarded-up building, nothing more than a wooden box really, with a roof made of corrugated tin. *Madam Marie, World Famous Psychic* is painted in big red letters on the side of the shack. We walk past Madam Marie's onto the boardwalk. I'm wearing Ivan's windbreaker with the hood pulled tight around my face. My short summer skirt whips up around my thighs. Ivan's wearing only a button-down and jeans, but the cold doesn't seem to bother him. He likes wet weather; the harder the rain, the better. It's the ambiguous days that depress him: when the sun is out but it's windy anyway, and the temperature wavers indecisively between hot and cold. San Francisco days, he calls them.

The rain has slowed to a drizzle, but the wind is roaring off the gray Atlantic so hard the boardwalk shifts beneath us. "Beautiful," Ivan says, leaning on the wooden rail to stare out at the ocean. "Could you live here?"

"Maybe," I say, but I'm thinking that it's colder here

on an April afternoon than any winter day I remember in
the city. I've never seen a beach so austere, just a narrow
strip of sand retreating from an angry ocean. On the Gulf
Coast the water spans out blue and bright for miles, but
here the fog hangs low and the world doesn't seem to
stretch much farther than my fingertips. I don't know if
it's mere habit or a slim attempt at apology that makes me
reach for Ivan's hand. He accepts, and we wander along
the boardwalk in the rain and fog. It's only a quarter past
two, but the sky is dark. I look over my shoulder every now
and then, half expecting to see Madam Marie plodding
along behind us, hands outstretched, her gold earrings
flapping in the wind.

"He called me once," Ivan says

I'm thinking about packing, wondering if Gristede's at
85th and Columbus puts its used boxes out by the curb. I'm
trying to calculate how many boxes I'll need to move out. I
estimate my life will fit neatly into four or five of the hefty
ones from the grocer, still smelling of apples from upstate
New York. That, plus a dozen or so smaller boxes from
Pricewise at Amsterdam and 81st, where the sturdy security
man in his creased pants and lopsided nametag always
greets me with a lifted eyebrow and a shout of "Hey Red."

"Of course I thought he'd call me," Ivan says. "I didn't
hear from him for a couple of weeks. But then one night
around midnight, I'm at home in bed. The phone rings
and I reach for it, and a voice says, 'Is Ivan there?'"

I'm so caught up in the logistics of our break-up—
when I'll leave, where I'll stay, whether or not I'll return
home, the failed daughter lugging boxes and books over
her parents' doorstep—that I don't realize where this
story is headed.

"'It's me,' I say. I'm half-asleep and I assume, at this point, that I'm dreaming, because it can't be who I think it is. 'It's Bruce,' the voice says. 'Sorry to call so late.' He keeps apologizing. He's worried that he woke everybody up, like he's going to get me in trouble or something. 'Look,' he says, 'me and my sister were just driving around. We were gonna get something to eat. Want us to come pick you up?'"

"You never told me this before," I say.

"Would you have believed me?"

"No."

"That's why I didn't tell you."

"Why now?"

"Because now it doesn't matter."

I wonder how long he's been holding on to this story, if it's something he made up a long time ago, or if he's creating it at this moment, one last desperate fiction to win me back.

"In the dark I grope for a T-shirt and jeans, pull on my Pumas, then navigate the carpeted stairs and creep out the front door. It's March in the Bay Area, midnight, which means it's kick-ass cold, and I'm standing out by the curb in the dark, shivering in my T-shirt."

Ivan is leaning against the rail looking out at the sea, raindrops running down his face. His hair is soaked, but he doesn't seem to notice. The top half of my body is dry beneath the windbreaker, but my legs are wet and frozen. I place a hand on his arm and try to pull him away from the rail, toward the car; he doesn't move.

"I wait for what seems like a long time, although it was probably no more than fifteen minutes. I see a pair of headlights down Balboa Avenue, but the car turns onto

Carmelita. I'm feeling really alone now, more alone than I've ever felt in my life, wondering what I'm doing on the curb outside my parents' house at midnight, waiting for the world's greatest living rock 'n' roll star to show up at my door. I tell myself it's a dream. As I'm turning to go inside I hear the low hum of a car engine a couple of blocks away. Then the headlights, and this time they turn down my street. The Mustang pulls up in front of my house. Bruce has the top down. His sister's in the passenger seat."

Ivan breaks away from the rail, turns, and jogs down the boardwalk toward our car. I follow. He unlocks my side first, then walks in no hurry at all over to his own. I'm shimmying into a pair of his sweatpants that I found in the back seat when he says, "There *is* a picture of us, you know. I wish I had it. I wish I could prove it to you."

"I thought you said there was no film in the camera."

"No, another picture. That night, we drove to Ken's House of Pancakes. We each got a quarter-pound burger with fries and coleslaw. I had a chocolate milkshake. While we were eating, Bruce's sister pulled a camera out of her purse. She was sitting beside Bruce, and she said to him, 'Go over there and sit next to Ivan.' He slid out of the booth and came over to my side and put his arm around my shoulders, like we'd been buddies for a long time."

He cranks the engine and a blast of cold air comes through the vents.

"Why are you doing this?" I say. "Why can't you just tell the truth?"

"I did tell my family the next morning. They didn't believe me. I've never told anyone since. I feel like those people from Roswell who claim to have been abducted. I don't blame you for not believing me, but at some point you just have to tell the story, no matter what people think."

Four days later, he helps me load my rented car. It's hard to know what belongs to whom, so I just take what I think I'll need: clothes, mostly, and books, my computer and VCR. The sleigh bed we bought at an antique store in Chelsea stays with him, as do three framed prints from the Stenberg Brothers exhibition at the MoMA. We hug and kiss goodbye. There's no animosity and, contrary to what I had expected, no feeling of relief. Just a big emptiness, the way I used to feel when I had to turn in my roller skates at Dreamland Skating Rink after a birthday party, knowing it would be a long time before I returned, already missing the feel of the floor spinning beneath me, the thud of the disco music on the loudspeakers. Leaving Ivan, I try not to think about all the ways I'm going to miss him.

"What if I track her down?" he says, adjusting my sun visor. "What if I find Bruce's sister and by some miracle she still has the photo? Then you'd have to believe me."

"This is pathetic," I say, buckling my seat belt. "It's not normal. What's wrong with the life you have? Why do you have to make things up?"

I have two thousand miles to convince myself that dishonesty is a suitable reason to end a relationship, forty-plus hours to rationalize my obsession with the truth. I think about all those trips he made to Quebec without me, and the ex's voice on the machine. "*Call* me," she'd whine, each time he returned from one of those trips, as if she had a right to demand this, as if she had some hold on him. What I wanted most from him, I guess, was satisfaction. I wanted him to think that what we had together was a sufficient story.

Driving over the Causeway into Mobile, I roll up the windows and close the vents against the gritty smoke of the

paper mill, that wet and sour smell. In high school we used
to escape the odor by burying our noses in plastic cups of
rum and Coke as we sped over the Causeway, headed toward the rowdy oyster bars and swank marinas across the
Bay. I wonder what happened to all those tall sure boys
whose fathers owned the boats I escaped to on Saturday
nights, boys who knew exactly how to position a girl on the
long vinyl couch below deck. The marina back then
seemed a sacred place, out of reach of Bay Street Baptist
Church and the Sunday School teachers who insisted that
my body belonged first to God and second to my future
husband. With the boats knocking against each other in
the dark, my hands guiding other hands beneath the
waistband of my jeans, I could almost believe my body belonged to me.

The heat is so intense by early April that it's difficult
to breathe. Still, the steamy humidity feels right in a way
New York's dry cold never did. I marvel at the calmness of
the bay, the enormity of the World War II battleship that
has hunkered there in the shallows for as long as I can remember. The traffic on the Causeway eases along, old
Cadillacs and Fords rumbling by with the windows down.
I'm already beginning to feel at home again in this region
of big American cars and pick-up trucks, bait shops and
motorboats. Tomorrow I'll drive down to the Gulf of
Mexico, lay out a towel in the shadows of the sand dunes
on the big public beach. It will be nearly empty, nothing
like Coney Island, and the water will be warm and tame
enough for swimming, nothing like the Jersey Shore. I'll lie
perfectly still and watch the sand crabs burrow into their
ramshackle holes, listen to their frenzied activity beneath
the surface of the sand. Then I'll walk down the beach and

count the disfigured jellyfish washed up on shore, their plump transparent bodies tangled in Sargasso weed.

As the Causeway grows longer behind me and Fort Conde looms ahead, the black cannons of the Revolution shining like playthings, I rehearse the speech I have prepared for my parents. I am certain they will be glad to see me, relieved that I have left "that awful city," which is the only name my mother has for New York.

At four o'clock in the afternoon I show up on their doorstep, haggard and half-asleep. I have to ring the doorbell like a stranger, because I no longer have keys to the house where I grew up. My mother answers the door. She's so happy she's laughing, until she notices my rental car in the driveway, packed so full the trunk is partially open, tied down with a length of rope.

"We liked him," she says over dinner. "David, didn't we like him?"

"You've been together, what, a couple of years?" my father says.

"Four," my mother corrects him.

My three sisters are grown and absent, pursuing lives in Georgia, Texas, and Tennessee. *Outward mobility* is the term my father uses to describe his daughters' slow but steady migration, one after the other until his five-bedroom house in Alabama's southernmost city came to resemble a storage locker more than a home. Each daughter's room, emptied of beds and essential clothing, contains plastic crates we keep meaning to go through, patterns for dresses we never made, shoes we can't bear to let go of, books we think we might learn from someday if we ever get the time: Darlene's American history textbooks from high school, Celia's French readers from

college, Baby's *National Geographic* collection, my Modern
Library series. Each of us left more behind than we took
with us when we moved. There is a feeling of absence
about the place, a lack of sound and movement all of our
messy possessions can't make up for. Alone with my parents for the first time I can remember, I feel the house the
way they must feel it: large and empty. With just the three
of us here, the table seems massive.

"Maybe you can patch it up," my mother says, passing
the peas over the wide expanse of glass. The table is sup-
ported by what looks like a giant conch shell, a monstrosity
of plaster and flesh-toned paint. *Mobile Bay Monthly* has a
name for this kind of table: Gulf Coast Chic. "Maybe you
should apologize. Maybe he really did meet what's-his-
name."

"Bruce."

"It's possible. Bruce puts on his pants, you know, just
like the rest of us."

"What's that got to do with anything?"

"You're almost thirty, I'm just saying."

Within a few weeks I have a job and a steady date,
someone I knew in high school who now works for his father's financial firm. In a couple of months the regression
is complete: I've purchased a tiny, refurbished shotgun
house on Church Street, half a block from the Mardi Gras
parade route. It's cute and it cost next to nothing. My
neighbors have frequent crawfish boils, to which I'm always invited. Some nights, they play Jimmy Buffett so
loudly his drunken lyrics must carry all the way across the
bay to Fairhope. A tall, sandy-looking boy from Murphy
High School mows my lawn in bare feet and cut-off Duck-
heads, taking beer breaks on my porch. He looks and talks

and moves like every boy I dated in high school, a Southern gentleman in the making, patronizing and smooth. When I invite him inside, he sits right next to me on the couch, so close I can feel the sweat of his thigh through my thin cotton dress. He invites me to spend a weekend at his parents' house on Romar Island. I am shocked to find myself flirting, tempted by the offer.

Nine months after the break-up a UPS truck parks in front of my house. The box is from Ivan. To the inside of the box he has taped a note. *Dear Gracie, I'm moving back to San Francisco. Found some of your things when I was cleaning out the apartment. Hope all is well with you. Love, Ivan.*

The box contains sundry items of no consequence: floppy disks with outdated software, playbills from a few off-off Broadway plays, a water glass from John's Pizza, a file folder labeled *Travel Ideas*, stuffed with glossy magazine photos of Iceland and Peru. There is a manila envelope full of photographs that inspire a nostalgia I'm not prepared for. By the time I'm finished looking at the photos—candid shots taken at subway stops, inside our crowded apartment, at B&Bs in the Poconos and Northern Vermont—I'm trying to convince myself that I don't miss him like crazy, that leaving him wasn't the last and worst in a long line of bad decisions.

The final photo is one I've never seen before, a grainy 5x7 in black and white, portraying a much younger Ivan with longer hair. He looks tired, as if he's just woken from an insufficient sleep, but at the same time he looks alive, more alive than I've ever seen him. The photo is taken inside a restaurant and has been shot from across a table. There is writing on Ivan's T-shirt, but I can't read it, because a bottle of ketchup intersects the small words. He's sitting next to a guy, someone whose face I know from other photos, from television and magazines. It's a wiry Bruce with a three-day beard. He's wearing a faded sweatshirt with the sleeves rolled up, and he's smiling half a smile, maybe a little tired, but happy. Their booth is in front of a window, and in the background I can see the darkness of the parking lot, and beyond the darkness the green glow of a neon sign announcing Ken's House of Pancakes. I search the photo for seams, for signs that it's been doctored, inexplicable alterations in light and shadow. I study the hand draped over Ivan's shoulder, its proportions and probabilities. I search for a hairline of space separating their two bodies, and, finding none, I marvel at the intricacy of the lie, the precision of the ruse, the bold lengths to which Ivan has gone to keep his story intact.

DADDY PHASE
Beth Ann Fennelly

we say,
as the child slaps the bottle from my hand
but opens wide for Daddy,

Daddy Phase,
perfectly natural, just a stage,
as she calls for him upon waking,
Daddy Phase as he rises to her, tired but flattered,
pretending I'm the lucky one, inviting me to keep sleeping

as if I care to keep sleeping
on the stale white bread
of this marriage bed, *Daddy Phase*—

me, I'm a huge bland lawn jockey
and she, she is a perfect
size zero, gigging the tireless horse of her father
back and forth across the kitchen tile

I think she just pretends to be a baby

I would like to pitch a fit
when she ducks my kiss
my lips two fat hot dogs
cooling at the drive-thru,

but would *she* bother to notice?
Would she feel *compelled* to empathize?
No,

because she's a BABY
it's a brilliant plan

A determined competitor, I
diversify my offerings

Have you seen this one? I ask her,

apparently she has

If only she still drank my milk
still drank my bloodwarm milk
then I could squeeze her, squeeze her, squeeze her

Oh there were entire years before she existed,
years of the single fare, years of the road trip,
years of the fishnets and the fake ID,
the Doc Martens, the come-as-you-are,
the backpack, hipflask, do-not-disturb,

I used to be a restaurant hostess Oh I had the power then,
tapping a pencil on my bottom lip
or slipping it whisperingly down the waiting list,
the tips that I palmed,
the gents that I stacked like quarters on a pool table—
one crook of my long red nail,
how they would leap to my side

but now,
now we're in the Daddy Phase

so now I remember

that each spring I'd discover
in the restaurant coat check room
some sad brown parka,
forgotten, forsaken—

so now I feel the elbows
of the empty wire hangers,
so now I hear them titter and hiss

LO, THE CHILD DISPLAYETH CUNNING, PARADISE IS FAYLING
Beth Ann Fennelly

Got her, trapped between my knees
after chasing her down the long hallway
where she's scampered with my lipstick,

when did she learn this snatch and ditch,
this mature desire, just last month she clamored
for nothing more salacious than ice cream

or another book before Night Night—
now she shakes me off—*You little brat*—
I'm prying each small claw from the silver tube

but she wasn't born yesterday and to prove it
head-butts my jaw, then kicks my kneecap,
Ah now I see it, the family resemblance

in her flushed and defiant profile, the same one
I marched past my mother in 6th grade
after 8th grader Jimmy Greenwood

lured me into the boathouse
on our school field trip, the oar of his tongue
scooping out the hull of my cheeks,

his hand sliding portside into my jean pocket
where yes I'd stashed my mother's stolen lipstick,
and my hand skating like a water spider

over the harsh and straining denim
of his fly, sizing up that other tube,
tube most forbidden so most ardently desired—

what power I took on with that knowledge
before the indifferent bus dropped me
at the end of our long driveway,

at least it seemed long to me then
when at the other end
the mother was waiting waiting to come out.

WAITING FOR THE HEART TO MODERATE
Beth Ann Fennelly

Adults had a drink, they said, *to take the edge off,* so that's
how she came to understand growing up: erosion. She was
all edges, on *tender hooks*, which is what she thought the expression was. Once she described this to her mother, and
her mother assured her it would pass. It kept not passing.
In a few years, she'd lie to her mother, drive to the city, and
wait in line beside the dance club, hugging herself beneath her growing breasts. What would this studious girl
do, once she got inside? Climb the risers and dance in a
cage. For her, it was not about alcohol or Ecstasy, at least
not the kind you bought. Under that strobe-light, the
music saw the music she had coming from inside and
raised her twenty decibels. She danced for hours, quelled
her frenzy a little. When she left, her ears felt cotton-
muffled, the Chicago streets hazy and desolate like a
movie without enough extras, her sweaty clothes stiffening
in the freezing wind.

She is twice as old as she was then, but here she is,
thinking that everything is yet to come. She is still the

chimney with its fire burning, and the sparrow trapped in the chimney. It's hardest in the caffeinated spring when her corneas are azalea-scorched, when the neighbor girls stroll to the Howorths' pool, unselfconscious, and flick the rims of their bathing suits which have crept a bit up their backsides. Watching from the window, the mirror, she knows she isn't one of them, though she still likes best the clothes in the "junior" section. Even having the baby hasn't moderated her as it might have. The sitter comes over, and they are wearing the same outfit. She knows her social-worker sister would call this *inappropriate.* She is by no means that slim young girl anymore, but how hard it is not to say, late into the party, *Let's toss our clothes aside, hop the Howorths' fence, and go nightswimming! Let's pile in some cars and race to the Gulf!*

Let's see. After the years of fevered dancing came the years of fevered travel (and all along, the fevered years of men), then the years of trying to settle in the town with the train that each morning would set the dogs to howling and set her edgy heart to howling alongside them. Now she lives in a town without a train, but it doesn't help. What helped: yesterday, she held her teething baby across her chest, and the child first gummed her collarbone and then bit, really bit, so hard the woman yelped. Six red crescents from the child's six teeth. For a moment, nailed to the here-and-now. And she loves the here-and-now! So why does she still want to dance all night? Why does she still feel music booming in her breastbone? Do others guess that something wild paces in this cage? She fears that, to free it, she might do something stupid.

MAKING AN EGG FOR CLAIRE, SUNNY-SIDE UP

Beth Ann Fennelly

I find a blood smear on the monstrous yolk.

Dead child, first love, there's a place for you, too,
at my table, but how shall I call you?
You died without ears in a town
so far away and cold with snow.

The Gods Tell Me,
You Will Forget All This
Beth Ann Fennelly

You lie, I answer. I remember circling the Q-tip dipped in alcohol around the stump of her umbilical cord. I remember the newborn diapers with the half-moon cut out so as not to chafe that black knot. Those hips the breadth of my hand. I remember the terror of trimming her nails.

No, they say, *you are forgetting. Already you have lost the trip to Indiana, when she was five weeks old. Tommy drove, you sat in the back leaning over her car seat because you needed to look at her as she slept or you would disappear—*

Sometimes even now I sit in the backseat with her—

It's different now. You sat in the backseat with her and you were sucking on a Tootsie pop—

Yes it was a cherry Tootsie pop

and although you knew it was wrong you touched it to her tiny mouth

I remember her tiny mouth

and she who had never tasted anything but breast milk

My breast milk

got the scent of that sweetness and her blind blunt tongue emerged and bumped against it, withdrew, bumped against it, withdrew.

Yes, that's how it was.

And you were fascinated at your own bad hand, holding the red ball there to her red tongue.

Yes, I was fascinated. Tommy heard my guilty giggle and looked in the rearview, so I lowered my hand. Later, we pulled over at a rest stop and I sat on a picnic table and suckled her, the yellow waffle-weave blanket over my shoulder, her tiny tummy warm against my own warm flesh. Afterwards, I hesitated, but showed him the Tootsie pop. He hesitated, then took it, held it to her lips and we giggled together. For months to come, when she was asleep and we missed her and it was all we could do to keep from waking her, he would imitate the tentacle-tongue slipping between the lips, not pointed with intent but flat, world-free, allowing the pleasure to meet it. Then retracting. Then emerging again. Ah, it was sweet, because she was so very small, and because it was our secret, our original sin, Claire's first solid food.

It was sweet because you understood you could hurt her and that made her more yours. And just yesterday you realized you hadn't mentioned that for several weeks so you said, "Do the tongue," but his imitation was off somehow. Though you both tried, neither of you could quite correct it. And so it is gone forever.

That's not true, I say. We'll recapture the tongue. Besides, I'm writing everything down.

That old lie. You'll look at the words and they'll crawl off the page.
But take solace that the pain fades too. You can't relive childbirth.

But I *want* to relive childbirth. I want everything back,
every blessed thing.

It's too much for one person.

Let me try.

You're too greedy. And it doesn't work that way. The infant is dis-
appearing as we speak. She is more ours than yours now.

Fine, I say, not meaning it. I'll have another.

THE WARSAW VOICE
Steve Yarbrough

"Poland isn't what it used to be," I tell Anna.

We're walking through the woods toward Tama Brodzka, which is only worth going to because there's a bar between the railway station and the bus stop. It serves beer, warm and on tap. I'm a frequent customer these days.

Off to the right, where Lake Bachotek lies, you can hear the calls of wild ducks. This morning, as Anna and her mother and I sat on the pier, a formation flew over, necks outstretched, bills wide open. Watching them swoop down onto the water, maybe a half-mile away, I wondered aloud where they'd come from. Basia said, "You seem to be thinking a lot about origins."

"I am," I said. "Don't you ever do that?"

"I do," she said, staring through the mist at the wall of woods across the lake. "Now maybe more than ever."

It began raining a few minutes later, so we climbed the hill to the lake house. Anna sat at the table on the ground floor drawing, and Basia lay down on her bed. I switched on the electric radiator, sat down beside it, and read a few pages of Shelby Foote's Civil War trilogy. I've brought all

three volumes with me—I reread them every few years—
and this time around I'm halfway through the second. I'm
taking my time. I don't know what I'll read when I finish
the set. I'm trying not to think that far ahead.

"Our money's running out," Basia said, still lying on
the bed.

"Toward the end at Vicksburg," I said, "Pemberton fed
his soldiers saddle leather."

"This isn't Vicksburg," she said.

This isn't Vicksburg and my wife's not a historian.
Otherwise she'd see that similarities abound.

*

The woods Anna and I are walking through are still
wet. Rivulets run down the sleeves of her raincoat, which
we bought on a Visa card the day before we left California.
Her sneakers, I notice, look soggy.

"What did Poland used to be?" she asks me.

"You couldn't buy anything," I tell her.

"Can we buy things now?"

It's not a simple question, but I pretend it is. "Of
course we can," I say. "Didn't we get those Legos down in
Warsaw?"

"I thought we bought them in Warszawa."

Once, a couple of years ago, one of my former col-
leagues asked her if she was bilingual. "No," she said, "I'm
Anna." She knows she's bilingual now, she accepts the fact
that almost everything has at least two names that often
sound nothing alike. But sometimes she has to be reminded.

After explaining that Warsaw and Warszawa are the
same place, I tell her that the first time I came here, back

in '85 when I met her mother, the stores were always empty, and usually there were long lines of people waiting out front.

"Why did they wait," she says, squeezing my hand, "if there wasn't anything they could buy?"

"They were waiting," I say, "because they kept hoping. They kept hoping something would turn up."

We break through the woods. Ten or twelve feet above us, beyond a metal guardrail, lies the highway to Torun. We walk along it for a few hundred yards. Cars whiz by. Some straddle the center line, others cut grooves along the shoulder. They're all doing about eighty-five or ninety. Some of the drivers have a full tank of gas for the first time in their lives, speed and power at the tips of their fingers.

Anna and I sit together at a table in the corner of the Universal Bar. A barmaid with the broad truculent face of a Polish peasant glares at us from time to time over the top of a translated Harlequin romance. Anna sips Pepsi, I drink beer. As usual, we're the only ones here. The place smells of cabbage, field sweat, and cigarettes.

"Daddy," Anna says when her bottle is empty, "why don't you tell me a story?"

She likes to hear them for the same reason I like to tell them: neither one of us knows how the tale will turn out.

"What kind?" I say.

"One about the guy who lived in Torun."

"The guy who learned the truth about the sun?"

"That's the one."

And so I tell her a story about Copernicus, whose green, dung-speckled statue she's seen standing before the town hall in Torun. "One night," I say, "Copernicus was taking a stroll along the Vistula. He was just a kid at the time, not too much older than you. A terrible disease had struck Torun. Back then, doctors didn't know some of the things they know now, and because they didn't, this disease had killed a lot of people. Copernicus's mother had just died, he himself had been sick, a lot of his playmates had died. He was trudging along without a destination. He just wanted to be close to the river. He wasn't looking at it, mind you, he was looking at the ground, but he could hear the water flowing, and he liked that rushing sound. It had been flowing for thousands of years, and it would be flowing when he went where his mother and his friends had gone.

"Suddenly, for some reason," I tell her, "he looked up into the heavens, and the night sky seemed to open up. He saw something big and round and incredibly bright. He just stood there gazing at it—it almost put his eyes out. Finally it vanished into nothing."

"It was the sun?" she says.

"No," I say. "Remember, this was at night."

"Maybe it was the moon."

"No, it wasn't that. He could see the moon too—this was something else."

"So what was it?"

"He never knew what it was," I tell her. "It might have been a cloud or it might have been dust or gas. Maybe it was nothing at all. Maybe he just imagined it."

"So what did he do?"

"What did he do?" I say, making a face as if I can't quite believe her question. "What do you think he did?"

"I don't know."

"He finished his walk," I say, "and then he went back home and took a nice warm bath and went to bed."

Now we're at the brink of revelation, and she knows it. She flattens her palms on the table and leans toward me over the empty Pepsi bottle. Her face is only inches from mine.

"So if that's all he did," she whispers, "why was what he saw up in the sky important?"

I take my time. I lift the beer mug and suck down some warm draft, then I stare out the door of the Universal Bar toward the bus stop where an old lady stands waiting. She cradles a little pig in her arms.

I set the mug back down and let my eyes meet Anna's. "Because," I tell her, "it got old Copernicus started looking up."

*

The resort at Bachotek is primarily for faculty at Nicholas Copernicus University in Torun. We're here because an old friend who teaches there arranged for us to come. He says the university is having trouble keeping the place open, so the manager, or Kierownik, takes in paying guests from outside. As a favor to our friend, Kierownik has agreed to a discount. He's under the impression that I'm on sabbatical.

We eat all our meals in a large hall near the pier. Each family has its own table, decorated with a plastic rose in a green glass vase. Until last year, I've been told, the roses were real. Then Kierownik opted for what he calls a one-time expenditure.

Just now, at supper, there are fifteen or twenty people present. Anna waves at Milek, her opponent in the competitions Kierownik stages daily for the children. Milek hollers "Hello, hello." He can speak a little English. His dad once spent a semester at East Lansing.

Basia spreads butter on a slice of bread and lays a single slice of cheese across it. She hasn't been eating much for the last few days. She hasn't eaten much for several months.

"I got a note from Kierownik this afternoon," she tells me.

I glance across the hall at the table where he eats. He's attacking a plate of spiced cabbage and sausage, his jowls flushed red from the effort. He doesn't look as if he's ever missed a meal. My friend in Torun says that right after martial law, when the shortages were at their worst, you could always eat pork for dinner at Bachotek. Kierownik, according to my friend, used to know all the local party functionaries. Now he knows all the priests. But mostly, I suspect, he knows himself, and he's a man who likes meat.

I say, "I had a coach back in Tennessee who used to eat like that."

"You can probably guess what the note was about."

"One time, at a Crystal on the way home from a road game, he ate thirteen burgers. Can you believe that?"

"I could believe anything," she says, "about somebody from Tennessee."

"Even me?"

"No," she says. "Not you. Not anymore."

"My boundaries have been determined?"

"Yes, and you've got some jagged borders."

This seems to me a fairly accurate assessment. I recall having made a similar judgment about myself not long after she met me, but she discounted it at the time.

"I assume his note was pleasant?"

"Extremely. He politely inquired how much longer we

planned to be staying."

I blow a stage-sigh out so loudly that Milek's father looks our way. "Onward Spartans," I say and wave at him.

If he understood me, he doesn't let on. He smiles, nods, and goes back to eating supper.

"I was afraid," I tell Basia, "that the note had suggested we pay up and take off."

"That's what it was doing," she says. "But you know that, don't you?"

"The thought crossed my mind, but I managed to chase it away."

"Can't we pay him?" Anna says.

"Of course we can," we both say.

"That's good," she says. Her bangs sweep low, hiding one eye. "I mean, I think he's awfully nice."

Afterwards, walking up the hill toward the house, she stays several paces ahead of us, as if she knows we need a little extra space.

"You're going to have to call California," Basia says.

You can't call anyplace from here. The other day we went to the office and attempted to call Torun, and it was more than four hours before the operator phoned back. Then we learned we'd reached a wrong number.

"From Bachotek?" I say. "That's impossible."

"That's why you like it here," she says.

"That's not the whole story," I tell her.

"What is the whole story?"

"I don't know the whole story," I tell her. "I remember a few scenes from the beginning, and the middle is fresh in my mind. As far as the ending goes, I'm blind."

She may yell, I think. She may yell like she did before I agreed to leave Fresno, when I lay on the couch all day long every day, the paper open on my chest, headlines screaming nasty news about the state budget. She may pull a branch off a tree and rake my face. She may tell me to jump in the lake.

Instead she takes my hand in one of hers and leans against me. When I travel from one continent to another, start eating different foods and bathing with locally produced soap, my odor, I've noticed, has a tendency to change, as if alien substances have altered my essence. Basia always smells the same. A little bit like apples, a little bit like wintergreen.

"You go to Torun and call," she says. "School starts in three weeks. If they haven't hired people back yet, they're probably not going to."

"And after I make the call," I say, "we'll know finally, beyond all doubt, exactly what to call ourselves. Temporarily laid off or permanently unemployed."

She pulls away from me. In the dusk her face hardens. "How about calling ourselves a family?" she says. "Did you ever think of that?"

*

"The Bachotek Olympics will now get under way."

Kierownik proceeds to prove it by jamming a round into the chamber of his pistol. The smallest kids, those in the two- and three-year-old groups, cover their ears and shriek. Anna pivots on one toe, Milek hops up and down like Ali used to do after entering the ring.

We're standing in a large shed not far from the dining hall. The shed has an asphalt floor and a tin roof, upon which we can hear the rain beating. There are no walls, and the wind blowing in off the lake is cold and gusty.

Milek's father and I stand near the kids, hugging ourselves, even though we're both wearing windbreakers.

"First event," Kierownik says, raising his pistol, "is the
fifty-meter dash. Two- and three-year-olds line up at the
chalk mark."

The rest of us stand there and watch the confusion
that results when Kierownik fires the pistol. One little boy
starts crying and runs up the hill toward the houses. A girl
turns and runs toward the lake. A few of the others take
one or two tentative steps over the line and then stop. One
kid, a plump little boy in red pants and green suspenders,
gets off cleanly with the shot and waddles all the way across
the finish line.

"A few years ago," Milek's father says, "I would have
said that we had just watched a future first secretary."

"What do you say today?"

"Today," he says, "I say that we have just seen a young
investment banker achieve glory in his first race. You'll notice that he appears to be the least athletic of all the
contestants assembled?"

"Also," I say, "the one least prone to distraction."

In the next race, for older kids, Milek could easily beat
Anna, but as usual he refuses to do it. They run as if
they're joined at the waist, bolting from the chalk line in
unison and crossing the finish side by side.

Cheeks red, chests heaving, arms around each other's
shoulders, they approach us, babbling a steady stream of
Polish, which I can understand if I want to. Right now I
choose not to, I let the words merge with the drumming
on the roof, with the sounds of wind whipping through
the pines.

At breakfast this morning, Kierownik passed out papers he'd picked up earlier in Torun—*Gazeta Wyborcza*, *Polityka*, *Zycie Warszawy*, and just for Basia and me, the *Warsaw Voice*, an English-language weekly that averages about four grammar mistakes and two misspelled words per column inch. I thanked him but didn't open it. Basia did. The first thing to catch her eye was an ad for a copy editor.

"The successful applicant," she read, "will be a native Pole with writing and editing skills in both English and Polish and a thorough knowledge of Polish ways and customers."

"I guess they mean customs," I said.

"I guess they do."

"I guess you think you might fit the bill?"

"Somebody has to fit some bill," she said.

"What bill do you think I fit?"

"I don't have an opinion. You're the only who can decide that."

"Funny to hear you say so," I said. "I don't feel like I've got the slightest control over it."

"If you don't have, who does?"

"A bunch of gray-haired guys in Sacramento."

She closed the *Warsaw Voice* and laid it down next to her teacup. "Yesterday afternoon," she said, "I did a little reading in one of your Shelby Foote books."

"Yeah? Did you check out the stuff on Vicksburg?"

"Actually, I did," she said. "I looked up the guy you mentioned. Pemberton. He had an interesting career. He was born in the north but married a woman from the South and fought for the Confederacy."

"You're saying I ought to fight for Poland?"

"Don't be a smartass."

"You're saying you want to fight for Tennessee?"

She stared at me as if I were the smallest form of life yet discovered.

"Well, if you're saying that I ought to fight for California," I said, "you can damn well forget it. It wasn't even in the Confederacy."

She picked up her fork. I didn't think she'd jab me with it, but I wasn't absolutely certain.

"After Pemberton surrendered Vicksburg," she said, "he was vilified throughout the Confederacy. There were those who actually suggested he'd lost the city and his army on purpose. Jefferson Davis didn't think so, but he couldn't risk giving him another command. So Pemberton resigned his commission as a lieutenant general and spent the rest of the war as a colonel of artillery."

It seemed only fitting at that moment to tunnel under her. It felt like the *thematic* thing to do. Besides, when you've sunk as low as I have, the only way you can move is by burrowing.

"That's in the second volume of the trilogy," I said. "If you'd looked into the third, you'd discover that Foote's final mention of John C. Pemberton occurs in connection with George Stoneman's raid on Salisbury, North Carolina. Guess what? J.C. surrendered again. Gave up every piece of artillery he had, every last shell, all his powder and his fuses. What sort of bill would you say he fit?"

Anna fits the bill of Olympic champion, at least as it's defined by Kierownik. In Kierownik's Olympics you get to mount the podium if you show up and stick around. While Milek's father and I stand by shivering, she and Milek record broad jumps of almost two meters, they hurl the frisbee at least three times that far. They complete the high hurdles—two overturned red buckets—in just under twenty seconds, breaking the old Bachotek record.

"And that record," Kierownik says, waving his pistol and causing nervous looks on the faces of the smaller kids, "was set way back when the president of our country was still soldering wires together in the bellies of boats in Gdansk."

*

Every Thursday afternoon there's an art class, conducted by a watercolorist from Torun. The kids gather in the dining hall and practice drawing and painting under his supervision, and in the evening the results are displayed on the wall near the kitchen and analyzed by the Kierownik while the rest of us eat. The artist who runs the classes says he thinks Anna has talent, though it's really too early to tell. Predictably, Anna's started saying she wants to be an artist too. When she asks me what I wanted to be at age five, I tell her I wanted to be a historian. That's true, as far as it goes. What I don't tell her is that I didn't want to be some of the other things I am. Unemployed, for instance. Incapable of supporting a wife who gave up a job she liked so she could come live with me.

Basia has promised to take Anna to the class today, but before she goes outside, where Anna's waiting in a fine gray drizzle, she says, "There's just one thing I want to say."

I'm sitting at the table, warming my feet in the heat from the electric radiator. I'm thinking that I've always loved rain. When I was a kid in Chattanooga, we lived on the side of Lookout Mountain, right above the Moccasin Bend. From there I could look straight down on the Tennessee, and when it was raining, I'd watch the river's rippling surface for hours, feeling snug and secure in my bedroom, thinking how lucky I was to be dry and warm, up there on the mountain rather than down in the cold deep river. Probably, if I want to be truthful about it, I've always feared falling into that river or one just like it. But the rain that swells the rivers is a longtime friend.

"You can either go to Torun tomorrow and call California or not," Basia says. "It's up to you. But Anna and I are leaving here."

"Going where?"

"Hopefully, somewhere with you. Either here or there. But we're moving out. Come Saturday morning, we're starting our forward march."

I glance out the window at Anna. She's wearing the pink raincoat. She stands underneath a tree, getting dripped on and studying the ground.

"You've told her," I say.

"Of course I have. She's started thinking this is her home. It's not. It's a resort. Normal people stay here a week or two. We've been here since June."

"You wanted to come to Poland."

"I wanted to get you *moving*. I wanted to get you off the goddam couch."

"You could have just dragged me up to Carmel."

"I wanted to be someplace where I can take care of Anna if I have to. Here I know how to get by." She opens the door and cold air rushes in. "Other people have lost their jobs," she says. "Did it turn them into plants?"

I watch while they slog down the hill toward the dining hall. The voice in my head is speaking Polish, and for once I can't seem to jam it. It tells me that of course Basia's right. Other people learn to call themselves by more than one name, they learn to do more than one thing. Baseball players dip below the Mendoza line and pitch in with the used-car salesmen, janitors, restaurateurs. First secretaries become investment bankers. Leonardo was a brilliant artillerist, Walt Whitman made a marvelous nurse. Jimmy Carter's a hell of a carpenter.

Hit men turn preachers, preachers turn pushers. A priest from Torun stopped the Earth and moved the sun.

*

At supper Basia's silent, her motions brisk and businesslike. She butters Anna's roll, she pours hers and Anna's cups full of tea. Mine is left for me to fill. I pour it about half full, though I know I probably won't drink it. I want to get a good night's sleep. The bus to Torun leaves Tama Brodzka at 6:45, so I'll start the day with a long walk through wet woods. I'll have an even longer walk, I imagine, tomorrow afternoon coming back.

Toward the end of the meal Kierownik rises. He taps a glass with his spoon, clears his throat, and gestures at the rear wall where the drawings from this afternoon hang.

"Ladies and gentlemen," he says, "it's time once again to examine the creations of our young artists. Judging from their past efforts, I would say there's an excellent chance some of them will have their work displayed in Warsaw one day or maybe even in New York or the cities of the American West." He nods briefly at Anna, whose cheeks immediately redden.

He starts with the drawings of the little kids, the two- and three-year-olds. "Here," he says, pausing before the first picture, in which two skewed circles, one slightly larger than the other, overlap, "we have a metaphorical representation of September 1, 1939. The artist titillates us with his title—'Big Ball, Little Ball'—but it's clear to any informed observer that the Big Ball in the drawing is Hitler's Germany and the Little Ball is Poland. The Big Ball is eating the Little Ball, but the deformation of the Big Ball—notice its squiggly borders, achieved by a very deft manipulation of the pencil—tells us that the Little Ball is already causing the Big Ball severe gastric disturbance. Here, of course, the artist comments upon the valiant efforts of the Polish army in the initial resistance to Hitler's war machine and at the same time skillfully foreshadows the Warsaw Uprising. The artist is both genius and patriot, and we marvel at the depth, the pure *historicity* of his vision."

He works his way through the whole series of drawings, spicing his analyses with references to Pilsudski, the Piast Dynasty, the Miracle on the Vistula, the Pope and the Black Madonna. Milek has drawn a turtle, which Kierownik says is nothing less than a symbol for contemporary post-Communist Poland: "slowly, inexorably putting herself back onto the right track."

Finally he comes to Anna's picture. It's a drawing of the Three Bears. They're holding hands, and she's arranged them by height. The biggest of the bears wears an orange sweatshirt on which Anna has written VOLS—a year ago, we went to watch Tennessee play UCLA at the Rose Bowl, and she must have seen such sweatshirts in the crowd. The middle bear is wearing a blowsy skirt. Anna's colored it red, black, green, and gold, in imitation of Krakowian folk design. She has dolls that wear dresses like that, and she saw a Krakowian dance group a few weeks ago in Torun.

The third bear is just a bear. She's naked, if you want

to put it that way. The most striking thing about her is that half her fur is white, and half her fur is black. The eye on the black side's white, the eye on the white side's black. It's as though she's part polar bear, part Smoky Bear, and thoroughly, unforgettably schizophrenic.

Kierownki, for a moment, seems troubled. He jams his hands in his pockets. His tongue pokes his jaw, as if probing for a weak spot. I measure the distance from where I'm sitting to the door, wondering how long it would take me to traverse it.

Then inspiration strikes him, you can see his eyes light up.

"Threeness," he says solemnly. "The Trinity. Its universal application. The utter indivisibility of it. Its importance in Poland and beyond."

*

It's my turn to put Anna to bed, so I climb the stairs to the attic. As soon as I slide under the covers, she says, "Daddy, tell me a story."

Lying there beside her in the dark, while the rain drums down and tree branches rub the roof, I realize I'm tired of telling stories, because stories, unlike history, need to have endings. And for me right now endings are a problem.

"A thousand years ago tonight," I say, hearing the sudden sound of Basia slamming a door down below, the wheels of a suitcase squeaking on the floor, "the king of Poland rode through these woods in a heavy rain just like the one that's falling now. He rode a big white horse. Beside him, on two more white horses, rode his wife and daughter."

"The queen," Anna says. "And the princess."

"That's right," I say. "They'd ridden a long way that day.

They had crossed the Vistula at daybreak, and they'd kept on going until they came to these woods and saw the lake and here on the hill above it a shelter. And when the king saw the shelter, he decided they would stop for the night."

"Why were they riding through the woods?" she says.

"They were fleeing a hostile army. The king's army had fought a battle against the foe and lost, and then the army had deserted the king. And the king was trying to make sure he and the queen and the princess got away to someplace safe."

"And when he saw the shelter here on the hill," she says, "he believed he'd found that place?"

"At least for the meantime," I say. "For that night, at least, he knew it was safe."

"And later?"

"Later," I say, "he might not get to be king."

"Did he know that?"

"You bet he did. He knew that one day soon someone else might decide to be king, and then he'd just be an ordinary person."

"Was he mad?"

"Not at all. He'd just about decided he was tired of being king anyhow. He was always fighting wars, some of which he'd started and some of which he hadn't, and he was always having to ride that big white horse, and the truth was horses scared him and he didn't like the way they smelled."

She cuddles up to me, so close I can feel her heart beating. "So what happened?" she says.

"That night? Nothing much. He and the queen and the princess went inside the shelter up here on the hill and they ate supper and got ready to put the princess to bed."

"Did the king put her to bed?"

"Sure enough," I say. "It was his night. And do you know what the princess said when he lay down beside her?"

"What?"

"The princess said, 'Tell me a story.'"

"And did the king do it?" she says, already sounding groggy.

"He did," I say. "This was the story he told her. 'Many years from now,' the king said, 'on a rainy night just like this one, a royal family found themselves up here on this hill. They didn't know how they'd gotten here. They had materialized, more or less, out of the air. That was how people traveled then,' he told her. 'One moment they were one place, one moment they were someplace else. In the course of their lives kings and queens and princesses lived in many different castles and ruled many different domains, some large, some small, some so tiny you could scarcely call them kingdoms at all. Sometimes,' the king said, 'a king might be a subject for a while, he might be an ordinary foot soldier, he might be a baker, a watchmaker, a puppeteer, the court fool. It wasn't always given to a king to rule.'

"'That night,' the king said, 'when the royal family went to bed, the princess asked the king to tell a story. And so he lay down beside her. And do you know what he said?'"

"No," she mumbles.

"'The king said, "A thousand years ago tonight, the king of Poland rode through these woods in a heavy rain just like the one that's falling now. He rode a big white horse. Beside him, on two more white horses, rode his wife and his daughter. They were fleeing a hostile army."'"

She isn't moving, so after a minute or two, I decide

she's asleep. But when I start to crawl out of the bed, she says, "Daddy?"

"What, honey?"

"I can't tell what's real in that story."

I almost tell her that I don't know either, that I don't know what's real in this story or in any other. But an answer like that won't satisfy her.

"What do you think's real?" I ask her.

She reaches up and pulls my head back down onto the pillow. Her eyes are open wide, and they're neither black nor white. In the darkness they look gray.

"The night," she whispers, "and the hill and the lake. And the king and the queen. And the princess and the rain."

LaPrade
Suzanne Hudson

The man rolled over in the dirt, a reddish-brown patch remaining on the left side of his face. Anyone could see that he had been crying, and he brought his fists up to rub the tears away, just as a child might. He made no move to untie the rope around his neck.

The sun was just coming up, edging its way through the ribbon of haze separating earth from sky. The haziness played tricks on the old man, mixing the greenery of spring with the blue that was always above it—or did it surround it? The man heaved himself into a sitting position to watch the rusted Studebaker raised on concrete blocks, a monument to a past he only remembered in distorted snippets. "Charmaine?" he whispered, then looked away, recognition lost.

The night's quiet still settled over the rotting wood and tarpaper shack, but soon he would hear Missy shuffling about, doing those things he imagined other women did in the morning. Boards would creak, then she would appear at the door. She would look at him and say, "You know you done bad, LaPrade." He would nod yes. Next she would put on the faded blue-and-red plaid dress that hung on the doorknob every night, walk over to the car, squat down beside it, and pee, holding onto the door handle to keep her balance. Finally she would come and untie the rope around his neck. He would promise to do better.

Missy was a lightly freckled mixture of child and woman, almost pretty when the light filtered just so, as though strained through a honey jar, melding the color of her eyes into an eerie echo of amber. Although her hair was brown, the light sometimes found a reddish tint, and the thick waves that spread out from a ponytail hanging down her back turned auburn at sunset.

She watched silently as LaPrade pulled some radishes for breakfast. She wore the green plastic bandeau he had bought for her at the Dollar Store in Isabella. It had a flower design cut into it. That made it extra-special. Over the last couple of years LaPrade had bought her more things than ever—a pop bead necklace and bracelet kit, some Romantique perfume, a ballerina pin (that was her favorite), comic books—"Archie," "Heart Throbs," "Richie Rich," and lots more. Every Saturday he walked the twelve miles into the little valley community of Isabella, bringing back some small treasure to occupy her for a while. Still, she knew that one swoop of his eyelid could reveal a soul unredeemed and threatening.

Missy didn't go into town with him often—people stared so—but once in a while she would go with him to the picture show, or the Farmer's Exchange, or to a drawing at the Sheriff's Office. Now that the child had come, trips to town were more rare. The welfare check had to go less for Dollar Store perfume and more for baby things. Missy slid the green-flowered headband off, then on again, combing a few loose strands of hair back with its plastic teeth. "You know why I done it, don't you, LaPrade?"

The man straightened up, folds of flesh on his otherwise gaunt body jiggling violently with every movement, even though his movements were slow and deliberate, as was his speech. "It makes me sad when you tie me out like that, Missy." LaPrade put the radishes in a metal pail and carried it toward the car.

The woman gave him a sharp glance, but hints of tears threatened to reveal themselves. "You was pinching the baby. I seen you do it. That ain't right. And the rope's your doing, too. Always has been."

LaPrade set the pail on the ground by the old car, sat down in a splintery, straw-bottomed chair, and began to lick the dirt off the radishes, spitting and scraping in the cracks with his fingernails. Finally he spoke. "I b'lieve you care more for that young'un than you do for me." The tears came again, just as they had the day before, the soul he was wearing dazed and helpless.

Missy put her arms around him, holding his face close to her chest. "I do so care for you," she said. "And you ought to care for that young'un, but I got to purnish you if you do it harm. I just got to." She loved LaPrade. She knew how to read him and how to tend to him, and he had needed tending ever since her mother died three years earlier—ran the car into the creek and killed herself. LaPrade had borrowed a truck and pulled the wreck out of the water, but he never found a body, and he hadn't been the same since. Missy loved him instinctively, the same way she loved her six-month-old child. She took care of them both. Yet her instincts were beginning to addle. At first she was sure that LaPrade would get over his anger about the baby, but the anger was growing into hatred now, and Missy was afraid—especially when she thought of how her father used to be.

"I ain't bad," the man sobbed.

"No, you're good, real good." Missy stroked his bald head, unconsciously avoiding the newborn soft spot.

The man turned, studied the car with smoke-gray eyes and a confused grimace, then reached out and ran his hand over the hood. Some rust stuck to his wet palm. He slowly brought the palm to his mouth and began to lick the rust, to make his hand clean, but he stopped abruptly with Missy's "I got to go see about the young'un." The man's sixty-year-old eyes followed the sway of the girl's hips, shrouded in red-and-blue plaid. His cracked lips settled into a childlike pout.

When she returned, the baby was at her breast. "LaPrade? You know tomorrow's Easter Sunday?" Missy was smiling. She always looked forward to Easter, when LaPrade would wake up before dawn to hide eggs. Exactly two hours later she would follow, dressed in her prettiest Dollar Store things, and begin to hunt. They would play hide-the-egg for days after, until the smell of rotten eggs, in hiding places that LaPrade had forgotten, filled the house and yard.

The wrinkles on the man's face rearranged themselves, settling around a sparsely toothed smile. "What do you want me to get you for Easter, Missy? I'm going into Isabella today."

"Get some of them plastic eggs—them kind that don't go rotten," Missy said. "I seen them at the Dollar Store. They're all colors. And you can take them apart and put other surprises in them. And we can play hide-the-egg all the time 'cause they won't go rotten!"

"What color eggs you want?"

"Green," Missy said. "And pink, too. I'm going to wear my pink pop beads and my pink socks tomorrow, so get pink!"

LaPrade stood up, stretched, then began to unsnap his overalls. "Missy, do you reckon we can do business now? Hit's been a spell." And his eyes showed her the shadow of malevolence that lived behind them if she refused.

The woman nodded yes, put the baby in a cardboard box next to the car, and lay on the ground. It wouldn't take long. No. Not long at all. It never did.

*

The red clay road wove its way down the side of the mountain for five miles before it turned into pavement. Missy always said that the county road to Isabella was ugly— no good scenery to look at—but LaPrade loved it. So skinny and gray without any of those white lines down the middle to bother a person's eyes. The way the trees coiled themselves over the strip of concrete gave him a sense of being sheltered from the rest of the world. It was rare that a car passed, and even less often that anyone offered him a ride, but he didn't mind. He didn't feel at ease with people—not even the few kin he had scattered across the county. Only Missy gave him comfort now. He loved his daughter. She takes care of me, he thought, watching with fascination as a small brown rabbit shot across the road, disappearing in the dark mass of trees and dank earth. "Yep, she shore does that. Takes real good care of me," he said aloud.

Green scents, black-eyed Susans along the edge of the road, and a feeling of Easter crept into LaPrade. Going to be a good walk, he told himself, just as he heard the soft sputtering of an engine from the hills to his back. Panic, as the old body jerked, trying to move in several directions at once; knees hitting hard on the pavement as he fell. LaPrade wanted to hide—run deep into the trees like that rabbit and hide. If only he could get far enough from the road before—but the black pickup was already in sight, beginning to slow down. Dammit, he thought, rising awkwardly. Don't want no ride.

"How you doing there, LaPrade? Want a lift?"

LaPrade grimaced pathetically, rubbing nervous palms over worn denim thighs. "Well, McCall, I just—"

"Oh, come on," the voice from the truck interrupted. "Hop in. No sense in you walking the whole way." McCall slapped the seat on the passenger's side.

The two men rode in silence for a long time, LaPrade staring down at his own hands, strong hands in spite of age, resting on his thighs. He would hurt McCall if he had to, if the man got too much into LaPrade's business. A car passed, heading in the opposite direction.

"Welfare lady," McCall noted, craning his neck to watch the blue convertible in the rear-view mirror. "Going to your place, you reckon?"

No answer. Missy will take care of it, LaPrade thought. She always did. Smart as a whip, that girl.

More silence; but finally McCall cleared his throat. "So tell me there, LaPrade—how's everything at your place?"

LaPrade's hand jerked. "Fine," he mumbled, without looking up.

And your girl Missy?"

"Fine. Missy's just—well—" He rubbed his hands together. "Missy's just fine," he blurted.

Silence, except for the sputtering truck, as green scents and sunshine blew steadily through the window against LaPrade's face, black-eyed Susans blurring along the roadside. McCall again cleared his throat. "To tell you the truth, LaPrade, I was hoping to catch you today. There's something—well, I figure we're neighbors and all, even if we don't live close by and don't talk much."

LaPrade could hear the blood pumping through his ears like a clock ticking frantically, low and loud.

"Is it so that Missy's done had her a baby? There's been talk of it."

LaPrade stiffened. There it was. The baby. He tried not to give McCall any sign of the hate—the intense hatred he felt for the child. Maybe if it weren't an arm baby it would be different, but the child wouldn't be ready for the ground for a long while. He could not stand to see Missy give her touch and time to anyone other than himself, but he did not dare change expression or McCall might suspect. We're kin, LaPrade told himself. We got our way of doing things. Why does anybody have to bother it? All because of that damn baby.

"All right," McCall sighed. "I just wanted you to know that there's talk. And there's going to be people looking into some things. Thought you ought to know. Is this okay?" he asked, stopping his truck in front of Stoner's Hardware Store.

LaPrade was startled by the heaviness of his body as he got out of the truck. He looked at his interrogator for the first time, mumbling a thank-you, and began his attempt to blend into the little town of Isabella, Georgia. He didn't see McCall staring after him, puzzling over such a crazy old man.

LaPrade chuckled at his reflection in the window of

Stoner's Hardware. I'm going to do real good today. I been bad. I know it. But tomorrow's hide-the-aigg. Out of the corner of his eye, the man could see a young woman walking beside and a little behind him. She was pretty, he suspected, because she wore a pink dress—Missy's favorite color—and she had red hair. LaPrade stopped walking as recognition came for the second time that day. Charmaine's hair had been red. Is it you? I done it. Done drove you away. You come back, you hear? Ain't going to do it no more. Ain't going to hurt you no more!

The roar of a cattle truck startled LaPrade, reminding him where he was. He could feel the perspiration on his forehead and the stares of passing people. He drew in his breath. Charmaine didn't enter his mind very often anymore, and he surprised himself when he did think of her.

The Dollar Store loomed before him. The words "Clary's Five & Dime" were still stenciled across plate-glass windows, although five-and-dimes were obsolete. Even the familiar smells hung over the store like the past it represented—month-old popcorn, stale chocolate and coconut, plastic things. The occasional ring of the antique cash register. The whir of the drawer shooting out. The wooden floor creaked as LaPrade made his way to the back left-hand corner where the toys were. Polka dot balls, Yo-Yos, and hideously grinning dolls cluttered the glass shelves. Dolls. Baby dolls. Babies. Their plastic eyes laughed down at him, and he glared back uneasily.

"Can I help you?" An elderly saleslady was beside him, smiling. LaPrade jerked his shoulders back, standing with all his weight on his right leg.

"Yes'm. I want to buy some Easter eggs."

"Easter eggs."

He cleared his throat. "Yes'm. Them kind that don't go rotten?"

"I don't think I understand." The woman's smile suddenly became artificial.

LaPrade shifted his weight to his left leg, nervously.

"Them kind you can put other surprises in. Them—"

"Oh." The woman relaxed, her smile natural again. "Straight back and to the right." She pointed to a large Easter display.

LaPrade stared at the pyramid of stuffed rabbits, yellow-and-blue baskets full of shiny artificial grass, marshmallow chicks, and candy—every kind of candy—and cardboard fans proclaiming, "He Is Risen!" LaPrade wished that he could take it all to Missy—make her forget about the baby.

He picked up some of the plastic eggs. Twenty cents apiece. He could get two green ones, two pink ones, and still have enough left for a chocolate rabbit—a little one. Missy'd be happy with that surprise especially.

Once outside again, the sun was bright, reflecting off the pavement in glittering patterns. LaPrade squinted. He felt very proud carrying the big green bag with "Bill's Dollar Store" printed across it. He couldn't resist peeking inside the bag several times during his walk home. The chocolate bunny stared back at him from deep within the green paper prison, through the cellophane cage, with eerily accusing orange candy eyes. It startled LaPrade, but knowing what a treasure he had was also comforting.

*

Missy had heard the automobile approaching long before it arrived. Now she and Mrs. Owens sat in the front seat. It was a convertible, looking brand-new. Missy loved the feeling of sitting in such a fancy car—even if it wasn't going anywhere.

"That sure is a pretty dress you got on, Mizres Owens."

The middle-aged woman smiled. "Well, thank you, Missy. Now if we can—"

"And that perfume smells real nice, too. LaPrade buys me perfume sometimes. I got some Romantique and—"

"Now Missy, stop all this." The woman leaned forward. "You know I didn't come here to chitchat about clothes and perfume and nonsense."

"Well, that's what ladies talk about, ain't it?" Missy whined.

"Stop it now. You're trying to keep us off the subject. Now behave." She paused, lighting a cigarette. Then, in a gentler tone, "I'd like to see your baby. Where is it? May I look?"

"No?" It was a half question. Mrs. Owens touched Missy's shoulder.

"Oh, Missy, honey, did it die?"

"No'm."

"You've got to show me sooner or later. You can get aid, you know."

"My baby don't need nothing from nobody."

"Is it a boy or a girl? And is it healthy? You know, child-birth is not without hazard if you do it alone, especially at your age. And if this is your father's child, there could be serious—"

"It ain't LaPrade's," was the calm reply, but the green-flowered bandeau was coming off and going on again, pushed back and forth by Missy's fidgety fingers. "Can't you mind your own business, please, Miz Owens?"

"Missy, you are my business. And I know you aren't stupid—you could better yourself. The most important thing is for you to be honest with me."

"Yes'm."

The older woman took a deep breath. "Now, I must ask you this question again. I'm just as tired of it as you are. But please. Please answer it honestly this time. All right?"

"Yes'm."

"Has your father ever raped you?"

"No!" The tiny voice began to rise. "He ain't never done that! And I told you—it ain't his!"

"Missy, you never cease to amaze me." Mrs. Owens calmly exhaled cigarette smoke through her nose, a menacing dragon with dyed hair. Her tone was harsh. "Now listen to me. I may be fairly new on your case, but I've learned quite a bit, so don't think you can fool me. I know you have not socialized with anyone, or even attended school for years. I also know you've got good sense. I just don't understand why you pretend otherwise. Could it be all these years of playing along with your father?"

Missy said nothing.

"Why did you quit going to school when your mother left? You were such a good student. Did he make you? Did he beat you? I certainly don't doubt that he beat your mother quite frequently."

"Miz Owens, Brother Claud told you them things, but he don't know. I swear he don't. We quit the Church a long time ago."

"You'd like to go back to the Church, wouldn't you?"

"Yes. I mean—no! They talk about me and LaPrade. I hate Brother Claud." But guilt was there. Missy began to cry.

Mrs. Owens touched Missy's shoulder. "It's not your fault. Don't you see he's always been a disturbed man? And he's getting old before his years, Missy. Feeble-minded. But we can fix that. Now, he's never done you any good. There are lots of agencies that we could—"

"You leave! Right now!" The bandeau was moving on and off more rapidly as Missy sobbed. "Why can't you people just leave us alone? We do just fine." She curled up in a ball next to the car door. This was different. Mrs. Owens had never before been so determined to make her change everything.

The woman lit another cigarette. She pulled Missy close to her. "Honey"—her voice became softer again—"honey, if you're doing just fine here, then why are you so upset?"

"You can't have my baby," Missy hiccupped. "And you can't—well, you can't take LaPrade and send him away from me nowhere."

"Don't you worry about that yet, honey. But do you worry about how he might mistreat the child?" She rested her head on the steering wheel for a moment, then raised it, looking, Missy thought, very sad. "Let me tell you one more thing, Missy." There was a small silence, then, "We think your mother is alive. It's not certain, of course, but she may be in Atlanta, using the name Charlotte Spurlynne. Here. I've written it down for you. Now why would your mother want to run away, do you think?"

For a second Missy wondered why she wasn't surprised. She spoke without emotion. "Well, she always liked Atlanta. And she was pretty. Real pretty. Lots of boys liked her, but there weren't nothing to it."

"Your daddy didn't like that, did he? Especially since

he was so much older than your mother. It made him mad, didn't it?"

"Sometimes. Sometimes he was mean to her, and sometimes she was mean. Sometimes LaPrade called her bad things. But she was a good Christian. Brother Claud said so at the memorial service. LaPrade ain't mean no more," she lied.

"How was he mean? Did he beat her?"

"I don't remember," Missy answered quickly, her voice rising. "Can't you just leave us be? He ain't mean!" she yelled, slamming her way out of the car.

Mrs. Owens threw the burning remains of her cigarette on the ground. "All right," she said calmly, shaking her head. "I'm leaving—for now, anyway. I think we've actually made progress today, but, Missy, if you just think about that baby of yours. Think about your mother. There's a lot we can do for all of you. Think about that, all right?"

The blue convertible soon disappeared down the red clay road. It didn't even take much time for the cloud of dust left behind to disintegrate. Missy stood and watched the burning cigarette until the fire reached the filter and it gradually went out. Then she went into the house to tend to her child.

It wasn't the house she had grown up in with Charmaine. That house was further up above the creek. There had been a kitchen table, some nice furniture, pictures of Jesus on the walls. LaPrade boarded it up after Charmaine was gone and forbade Missy to set foot in it again even though he visited it every once in a while. She had not allowed herself to miss it much until now.

Their present home was an abandoned shack with a

sparse kitchen, a crude shower, and a shithouse down a trail near the creek. But it was enough for LaPrade. She knew to go along with him over the years, keep him from turning on her. Be a good daughter. But I am fifteen now—like mama when I was born. And now I am a mama, too. Missy sat in the doorway of the shack, the baby at her breast. She could see LaPrade walking toward her about half a mile down the road. "Yonder he comes, baby. Bringing Easter eggs. You like that?"

The child replied with passive sucking noises. "He's a good man," she said, then whispered, "Oh, I know he's bad from time to time—like pinching you. He just needs to be took care of." She reached up, touched her bandeau, and thought about how nice LaPrade was to buy her pretty things. She didn't like to punish him. It wasn't any easier now than it had been the first time—the day after he had given up the search for her mother's body. She had been twelve then, confused by the man her father was becoming and the strange changes in her parents over the years. But he had begged her. "I thought some lies about Charmaine," he had whined, like a little boy. "I'm bad. You got to purnish me, Missy."

She had been frightened. He had always done the punishing, the beating, the deciding of everything. But he was handing her a rope, begging to be punished for his wife's death. At first Missy had thought he wanted to be hanged, but she couldn't do it and he didn't have enough left within him to do it himself. Terrified, she had solved the problem only by using the first thing she noticed—an old, but sturdy, fence post. One end of the rope around the post, the other around her father's neck. Missy's night, alone in the house, was filled with intermittent sounds of LaPrade's guilt, occasional thuds, and cries of pain as he ran out the length of the rope and was thrown to the ground.

"Charmaine, you can't be dead!" he would scream. "You come back here! I ain't going to say no more! Nothing about Fred Culver or Adon McCall or none of the others! I ain't! I swear to God I ain't!" Those words had become more jumbled as the night moved into dawn. Finally she had crept out of the house and held him next to her— pitied him—done business with him. It was her obligation. She was kin. She accepted it. It was a sacrifice—a Christian sacrifice; any guilt that crept in she learned to dissolve. It was a matter of survival. These days she was coming to see that her own child must also survive.

"Baby, you sure are pretty." Missy spoke aloud again. "Just like my ballerina pin. Sort of hard to tell you two apart."

The screen door squenched loudly, slamming behind her father. "Wait'll you see!" LaPrade cried, laughing. "Wait'll you see!" he sang over and over, dangling the sack in front of Missy's excited face, dancing around in crazy circles.

"Give it, give it!" she squealed, laying the baby on the floor, chasing LaPrade outside and the fifty yards to the creek, where he collapsed in the weeds, hugging the bag to his chest.

"You know you cain't see till tomorrow."

"Well, I reckon I will see tomorrow." Missy was too out of breath to play any longer.

"You take care of that welfare lady today?"

"Told her to let us be," she answered, wondering if she should try to share her thoughts with him. No, she decided, I ain't going to spoil no Easter Sunday. I can let him have that, can't I?

"I thought about Charmaine today," LaPrade said. "There was a red-haired woman looked just like her in Isabella." He scratched his elbow. "Missy? What you reckon made me call her all them names? She didn't—"

"Hush up!" The woman looked at him sharply. "Now don't you go feeling bad, and don't you go crying. Tomorrow's hide-the-egg."

He nodded and gazed blankly at the creek, mumbling, looking helpless the way he did from time to time. So different from the angry, accusing father of her childhood, who drew blood and defiance from her mother as Missy huddled in corners praying for God to make him stop. Missy shivered as a phantom rabbit scooted across her grave, reminding her not to think forbidden thoughts. She was beginning to get to know her mother much better.

"Come on, LaPrade." Missy took his hand and led him back to the house; she would cheer him up. They would giggle and tease one another, plan for hours about Easter. Then she noticed the baby on the floor, felt the uneasiness again, and ran to comfort it.

*

A good day for hide-the-aigg, LaPrade thought as he crept out of the little house, careful not to disturb Missy. Outside, the mist took on a yellowish cast from sunshine soaking through green leaves. Fresh dew on clumps of grass made it look like the artificial Easter kind at the Dollar Store. Pretty, he told himself, reaching for the eggs in the big green bag. Missy'll be so happy.

The man gently carried the two pink eggs over to the old automobile. It would be a perfect hiding place. Giggling like a little boy with a secret, he put the first egg behind one of the concrete blocks supporting the vehicle. The second went under the front seat. "She'll never find that one," he chuckled. A green egg was situated in a clump of grass by the house. The man praised himself for being so smart about mixing the colors. LaPrade stood still for a long time, thoughtfully searching out a hiding place for the last egg. As his eyes rested on one of the peeling pieces of tarpaper, he smiled. I done good, he told himself as he wedged the egg behind the flap of paper. A few termites emerged from holes in the wood.

"You just can't figure out what that big old green thing is, can you?" LaPrade said to the frantic insects. "Well, this is the best hiding place ever, so don't you go messing with it." He laughed at himself. "Talking to bugs," he muttered.

Now it was time for the real treasure. Slowly, ceremoniously, the old man took the chocolate rabbit out of the cellophane. He set the candy animal in the radish patch, proud of himself for being so smart about it. The orange eyes seemed to follow him as he went back into the house.

She'll be awake soon, he thought, almost tripping over the baby. The child gazed up at him blankly, not making a sound. LaPrade had a sudden urge to crush it—place his foot on the child's tiny body until all life was gone. No, he told himself firmly, that would be bad, and Missy likes it. Likes to play with it. Suddenly, LaPrade had a wonderful idea. I'll hide the baby. He began to get more excited. Missy's gon' love this game. He clumsily lifted the child, stiff arms held out from his old body. It still didn't make a sound—but then, it hardly ever cried.

By the time he returned, the woman was standing in the doorway—all blue-and-red plaid and pink.

"I never seen you looking so pretty, Missy."

"You think so? You think my pop beads look good? I was going to mix some blue in with them, but pink's such a pretty color all by itself." She looked at him expectantly.

"It's fine, Missy. You're prettier'n ever."

"LaPrade?" Missy walked toward him and touched his elbow. "Where's the baby? I couldn't find it when I waked up." She must not show anger, must not confuse him or rile him. She knew the danger in that.

The man smiled. "Don't you worry. I done moved it. Right now you got to hunt the aiggs!" he exclaimed.

The woman hesitated, then giggled, knowing that she must, and immediately ran toward the car. "You always hide one here, fool." Laughter. Green and yellow sunshine. It went by much too quickly to suit LaPrade. He was disappointed when, after the last egg was found, Missy again asked about the baby.

"Missy, I can't tell. You got to find it—like the eggs. It'll be fun!" But Missy wasn't smiling. That wasn't supposed to happen. She was supposed to be pleased.

"You better not have hurt it, LaPrade," she said evenly.

"Missy, now don't be mad. It's a game. It's—" He stopped, afraid of the way she was looking at him.

"You tell me where it is. Right now, you hear me?"

The man slowly turned his face toward the car, then the creek, then back to Missy. He began to cry.

"I done forgot," he sobbed.

The woman froze, not believing. "No," she whispered, then screamed, "What did you do to it?"

LaPrade looked thoughtful. "Don't worry, Missy. She ain't dead. I seen her in Isabella yesterday, remember?"

But his daughter wasn't listening. She was running—

running hard, pushing through morning-moist green leaves, head jerking frantically left to right, searching. *Where you at, baby? You under that old car? LaPrade. He ain't right, Mama, but you lied and I need my young'un.* Missy was breathless, sobbing, running from car to house to clumps of trees and back again. There was not enough of her to get to all the places the baby might be.

She lifted the hinged door set in the floor of the shack where LaPrade stored potatoes and moonshine. But at once she realized she had already looked here, her panic pushing her into a randomly repetitious search of only the most obvious places: the shithouse, the old car trunk, a kudzu-covered aluminum boat, the washtub where she had bathed her old doll babies only a few months before, Frantic phrases throbbed through her brain. *Baby ain't no doll. Baby's real. Ain't no plastic toy. Baby can die. LaPrade killed it? No, please. Need my young'un. Got to be it. You done made a choice, Mama. Mama.*

Suddenly Missy knew. She began to run the fifty yards towards the creek, the word *mama, mama, mama* drumming through her head, setting a cadence for her breathing. She saw it as she approached the water. A tiny, mud-caked child, making strange little choking sounds.

"Oh, baby," she whispered, gently picking it up. "Baby, poor baby," she cooed over and over, softly, as she walked toward the house. Mizres Owens must be right. It must be so. As Missy wiped the mud from her baby's face, she knew.

LaPrade was exactly where she had left him, only he was sitting now, rocking back and forth, crying, "My fault, my fault."

"You could've kilt it!" Missy said sharply.

"Oh, Missy, I ain't—"

"You could've kilt it! Just like—well, just like you could've kilt Mama."

"But she ain't dead," LaPrade said. "I seen her in Isabella."

Missy sighed. "You just ain't right, LaPrade. Now you know what I got to do?"

The man obediently walked over to the old fence post and allowed Missy to tie the rope around his neck. She sat in the doorway of the shack and stared at her father for a long time, glancing occasionally at the rusty automobile. She held her child close, reaching up every now and then to comb loose strands of hair back with the plastic headband. "You know what we got to do, baby?" she whispered. The child merely gazed up at her, some dark mud still caked around its neck and face. The woman sighed, stood up, and went to LaPrade. She gently kissed the top of his bald head. "Goodbye, Daddy." She stroked his cheek. "I got to do it. I just got to." But she was walking uncertainly down the dirt road away from the shack.

"Where you going, Missy?"

She stopped. Turned around. "Leaving." Tears were finally allowed to touch the faint freckles on her cheeks.

"You cain't!" LaPrade screamed. "Where you going?"

"Don't know," she sobbed. "To see Mizres Owens. Maybe to Atlanta."

"You don't know what you're doing!" The man called out. "Look here, Missy. Look here what I got you. In the radish patch. Look here. A candy rabbit!"

The woman hesitated, then continued walking. "Done made my mind up, baby. Ain't no candy rabbit going to change it," she mumbled.

"Missy!" he yelled, running out the length of the rope,

feet rushing from under him, falling hard on his back against the dirt. "I ain't going do it no more!" he yelled louder, pounding his fists in the dirt. "I promise! You don't care nothing about that young'un. It ain't even got no name! Missy!"

The woman stopped abruptly. After standing very still for what seemed like a full minute, shoulders rising, falling, rising, she turned one last time and screamed, "William! Its name's William!"

The man lay in the dirt. She was out of sight now. Had been for quite a while. LaPrade's gray-filmed eyes gazed blankly at the chocolate rabbit. It was beginning to melt, and the orange eyes were sliding down the dark-brown cheeks. By mid-afternoon it was covered with ants and flies and even a few yellowjackets.

WHITE TRASH FISHING
Ron Rash

When the necktie around my collar feels like a noose, and I'm weary of air-conditioning and fluorescent lights and people who never say "He don't" or "Co-Cola"; when I find myself in agreement with my NASCAR-obsessed cousin who claims if it ain't got wheels it ain't a sport; when Pabst Blue Ribbon tastes better than Guinness and I want to drink it in cinderblock death-traps with names like Betty's Lounge and The Last Chance; when I hanker for pork rinds and those deviled eggs you barehand out of a gallon jar; when I tire of eating animals and (yes, my dear vegetarian friends) plants that someone else has done the messy business of killing for me; when my wife says what's got into you and makes clear whatever it is is no good thing; then I begin to long for muddy water and fish with poisonous fins and faces like nightmares, and I know there is only one thing to do: I haul a rusty tacklebox and two Zebco 404 rods and reels out of the basement and go white trash fishing.

What I'm talking about is nothing like trout fishing on the Beaverkill, or Henry's Fork, or in the Smokies, or the spring creeks of Pennsylvania or any of the other meccas of the sport where men and women with fly rods pose mid-stream as if on the cover of an L.L. Bean catalog and would no more harm their catch than than their dogs or children.

What I'm talking about is not largemouth bass fishing either, especially its current manifestation as symbol of the New South: a high-tech sport requiring sonar and radar equipment as sophisticated as a nuclear submarine's installed on boats swift as some airplanes so the angler can zig-zag across the monstrous reservoirs that fuel the New South and thus compete with hundreds of other fishermen similarly equipped in championships where fish are kept in a livewell until weighed, photographed, psychoanalyzed and who knows what else before being tossed back or mounted on a wall.

What I'm talking about is killing what you catch and eating it right there on the riverbank. And I'm talking about a river, not some gin-clear stream or reservoir, because that's where white trash fishing is best done, a river where the water's the color of coffee with cream and a trout or bass would go belly up before it swam five feet. I'm talking about sitting on a riverbank littered with beer cans, bait containers, potato chip bags, used diapers, used condoms, rotting newspapers, rotting blankets and just about anything else you'd care (or not care) to imagine.

It really doesn't matter what the place looks like because I'm talking about night fishing and even if the place looked like the Yellowstone River I wouldn't be able to see it anyway. The only reason I'll even be here while the sun's still up is to stake a claim to a spot and get the rods and reels rigged up and the Coleman lantern and stove set up, fueled, and primed for later.

And this is what else I bring: frying pan, corn meal, Crisco, and onions, a mess kit, a cooler filled with ice and PBR, bug spray (though it doesn't do much good), a sleeping bag, a plastic tarp in case it rains, a pistol, the bait, and, of course, what I'm wearing.

And this is what I wear: a cap that says Catfish Fisherman Do It All Night or I Don't Care How They Do It Up North and the rankest jeans and shirt I can scrounge up out of the attic or bottom drawer, because even if I don't catch a fish the bait will leave a permanent reek on my clothes. Because what I'm talking about is that I'm after catfish, the aquatic equivalent to a possum in that they will eat anything they can grub up off the riverbottom. There is no concern about "matching the hatch" or whether to use a green or a white skirt on a spinnerbait. If a catfish finds it, it'll eat it. The problem is it's moving blind down there, especially in the middle of the night, so I've got to help the fish out by giving him something he can smell. What I'm talking about is purple nightcrawlers threaded on a hook like shish kebab. What I'm talking about are doughballs textured with anything from motor oil to ketchup. I'm talking about whatever will get the job done.

When the sun finally goes down it's time to bait the rigs and cast into the dark and listen for a splash to know I didn't snag a willow. Then I sit down on the bank or a stump or maybe a lawnchair someone left, take a beer from the cooler, and wait.

It might be a while, but when I feel tugs from the dark more insistent than the current, I tighten the line and jerk for all I'm worth. I'm not talking finesse here. The object is not giving the fish "a sporting chance." What I'm talking about is setting the hook hard enough to drive the barb into the fish's brain and settle it once and for all right then. I don't "play" the catfish until it tires: I've got thirty pound test line and unless the fish wraps it around a junk car or refrigerator (and yes, there are cars and refrigerators down there along with anything else someone could throw or push into a river) it's not going to break the line, so I reel it in quick as I can and heave it onto the bank. I'm not talking about second chances when a fish flops back into the water when the hook is taken out—I'm talking rocks, tire irons, anything that can whack the fish into a limp silence.

And after I've caught enough I skin and clean the fish then put the frying pan on the stove and roll some chopped-up onion and corn meal into something that looks a lot like what I've been fishing with to make hush-puppies and then I lay the catfish in the pan. I get another beer from the cooler and when the last fish is fried I sit there and eat and sip the beer and listen to the frogs and the crickets and the river itself as it rubs against the bank. And when I finish I unroll the sleeping bag. I take out the pistol and fire off a round at the sky to keep anybody else on the river at a distance. Then I snuff the lantern and sleep so deep it's like I'm under the river, not beside it.

Come mid-morning the sun filters through the trees and I wake up. I'm cotton-mouthed and swollen with mosquito and chigger bites. I'm sweaty and smelly, my hands and clothes sticky with bait and fish slime. My head feels like somebody with a tire pump stuck the needle in my ear and didn't quit pumping until he'd doubled my hat size. But that's OK, because I will feel cleansed and somehow redeemed as I stumble up the trail to my car.

THE ONES WHO ARE HOLDING THINGS UP
Jennifer Paddock

November 1986
Chandler

Leigh is the kind of girl who hangs around girls who get in fights. Not that she wears rock concert T-shirts, but she does smoke. She and I are different, but we are friends. She's been to my house, three stories with woods and a lake in back, a game room, halls you can do cartwheels down. And I've been to her house, dark and small and sad.

Sarah is beautiful and theatrical and is my best friend and has been since the day I almost killed her. When we were eight, she talked the assistant golf pro into letting us hit range balls, and she walked right behind me on my backswing. There was screaming and blood and an ambulance, and seventeen stitches to the back of her head in the shape of a C, my own initial. Then we began taking tennis lessons and now are known as *those tennis girls*. A tournament can get us out of school for a week. We go to a public school and make good grades without studying. We are on the outside of the inner circle of cool kids but are cool enough.

I'm in Spanish class zoning out, not listening to the scratchy record of a Mexican family having a conversation at breakfast. I'm thinking about my plan for lunch today with Leigh and Sarah, maybe at the country club, and wondering how that would go.

My father tells me that where we live, in Fort Smith, Arkansas, used to be called "Hell on the Border." It was a place people passed through: Cherokee Indians on the Trail of Tears, gold miners to California, trappers canoeing up-river, ranchers headed to Texas, outlaws seeking freedom.

I imagine there are worse places to grow up, and I am lucky to be rich and to love my parents, but I do not love it here. I will pass through.

Between first and second period, at my locker, I see Leigh at her locker, tapping a pack of Camel Lights, and when she catches my eye, I start to walk over, but somebody, a real genius of slapstick, comes up behind me and pushes the back side of my right knee, causing my leg to buckle, and I almost trip. I turn around with a little agitation and find Sarah smiling her coy Sarah smile.

"Falling apart at the seams, Chandler?" she says. Then Trey, the running back, rushes Sarah, taking her in a head-lock, holding her like he's in love, and I wonder if Sarah notices this, and when he lets go, there is purple dye smeared across his white jersey. Sarah is always dying her hair. She probably just did it thirty minutes ago, staying home during first period, using one of the drawerful of late notes her mom has written for her.

I watch Trey pushing Sarah down the hall.

"Trey's walking me to class," Sarah yells back. "I'll meet you on the court."

Second period Sarah and I have gym, and so does Leigh, but Coach McGavin lets Sarah and me play tennis, while Leigh and all the other girls have to square dance with the PE boys. I look around for Leigh. I know she has a car today because I saw her pulling into the lot in her mom's old Chrysler, a two-tone two-door.

Sarah and I aren't sixteen yet like Leigh is, even though we're all in the tenth grade, so every day we try to find an older kid with a car to take us off campus for lunch. We've never asked Leigh to take us because you never know when she's going to have her mother's car. Mostly we ask this sweet guy who's a senior in the band, a trombone player, and sometimes we go with this swimmer girl who's a junior with a Bronco. If we ask guys, we always ask guys we would never want to go out with. It would be too humiliating to beg for a ride from a senior on the foot-ball team like Trey. But I don't see Leigh anywhere.

I'm late to gym, but I don't mind. I actually prefer it because I hate undressing in front of the other girls. It's not that I'm overweight or ugly or anything. Though I'm cute enough and have blonde hair, I'm shorter and look younger than the others, with smaller hips and breasts. At home, everyone is always covered up. My mother wears a pink or blue cotton nightgown and a pink flowery robe, and my father wears neat Brooks Brothers pajamas with a tattered terry cloth robe that used to be brick red, but is now pale with spots from too much washing.

Sarah likes undressing in front of other people. When I spend the night at her house, she'll walk down the hall from the bathroom to the bedroom, naked and thin, her straight past-the-shoulders hair hidden under a towel knotted in front, and when I stand there frozen, watching,

Sarah says, "What?"

I see Sarah already on the court, sweatpants on, her lucky blue Fila jacket tied around her waist. She's hitting her serve so hard that it bounces in the square, then flies to the metal fence with a clang. My serve takes a couple bounces before it hits the fence with barely a rattle. I can still beat Sarah, though I know it's only a matter of time until she learns to play more consistently, eases up on her power, mixes up her shots. Right now it's a head game—our matches are close, but I always win.

When I was nine, I went the entire summer, at least ten tournaments in all parts of Arkansas, beating my opponents, even Sarah, 6-0, 6-0. I'm so dreamy about the days when I used to kill everyone.

Sarah and I play a groundstroke game to eleven. I win, barely, by hitting the same shot, deep with topspin, every time. I really do get into a kind of rhythm, and I start thinking of myself like a Buddhist monk chanting *one two three hit* or like my father who meditates saying the same secret word over and over.

Afterward, we fill up an empty tennis ball can with water and take turns drinking and talk about what we're going to do for lunch.

"We could stay here," I kid. "Get a Coke and an ice-cream sandwich and stand outside."

"Ah, Chandler baby, no," Sarah says, and I smile.

We start walking back to get dressed for third period, and I spot Leigh smoking under the stadium bleachers. She's long-limbed and awkward there in the shadows but has a pretty face, her wavy brown hair pulled back by two silver barrettes.

I twirl my racquet twice and catch it on the grip. "Why

aren't you inside square dancing?" I ask.

"They don't ever miss me," Leigh says.

"Can I have one of those?" Sarah says, then sets her racquet and the tennis balls on the ground.

"Sure," Leigh says, like she's honored that Sarah would smoke one of her cigarettes, and lights it for her. Sarah and Leigh don't really know each other, only a little about each other through me.

"Hey, Leigh," I say, thinking about my lunch plan, and I take the rubber band out of my hair, letting my ponytail fall. "Did your mom call in sick?"

Leigh doesn't answer, just gives me a look like she's ashamed.

"I don't mean anything by it," I say. "I just wondered if you have the car today?"

"I have the car."

"You're sixteen?" Sarah says.

"Yeah, since October." Leigh pauses a moment, taking a drag and looking at us. "Why, do y'all want to go to lunch?"

I smile. "That'd be great. Thanks, Leigh." I reach out for a smoke, and Leigh lights my cigarette off hers, then flicks hers away.

Sarah lets her hand fall to the side and drops her half-smoked cigarette in the grass. "So, how about Hardscrabble?"

Hardscrabble is the name of the country club where Sarah and I have spent nearly every day of our lives playing tennis. I used to think the name was a golfing term, but my dad told me it's because the golf course used to be a farm, which was known, because of its rocky conditions, as a "hardscrabble" way to make a living. It seems weird to me that it's a name of a place where rich people go to take it easy.

"Definitely," I say. "Hardscrabble."

"Do we have time?" says Leigh.

"I have study hall next period," I say. "I can call in our order. No problem."

"But I'm not a member," Leigh says.

"We know, and we'll buy," Sarah says. "What do you want?"

Leigh gathers her hair in her hand, then lets it go. "Maybe a turkey sandwich. With bacon."

"You mean a *club sandwich*?" Sarah says.

"I guess," says Leigh.

"All right, Leigh," I say. "We'll meet you in the parking lot right when the bell rings. We have to beat everyone out and get there, or we'll never finish in time. It's like a sit-down dinner."

"I know," Leigh says. "We'll get there fast. I'm a good driver."

"Then we'll see you later," Sarah says. She picks up her racquet and the can of balls and walks away, and with the cigarette in one hand and my racquet in the other, I follow.

In study hall, all the football players sit in the back and never study. The closest they come to any real work is copying assignments from me or any other humanitarian who will let them. Trey is always goofing off and thinks it's funny to hold up notes written in big letters that say something like, "Hi, Chandler." I always smile when he does that, even though I know it's subnormal.

Trey and I went to the movies once, and he called my house right before he was supposed to show up and asked my dad, who rarely answers the phone, to ask me if I would iron his shirt for him. My dad was laughing and yelled the message up to my room, and I yelled back that I would. And when Trey came to the door, my dad actually answered because he said he wanted to meet *this* boy. Usually, if I had a date, my dad would run and hide in the kitchen and leave my mother or me to open the door. It's not that my dad doesn't care about who I go out with. He just doesn't know what to say. And neither did Trey and I on our one and only date.

Coach McGavin runs the study hall. What an easy schedule he has—gym and study hall. I walk up to him, and he gives me the pass before I even say what I want it for. "Thanks, Coach," I say. I go to the pay phone and call Hardscrabble's clubhouse, where we like to eat lunch. They also have a snack bar, but it's not nearly as nice as the clubhouse. I order a club sandwich for Leigh and two French dips for Sarah and me. I tell the guy who answers to have it ready at 11:30, that we're coming from school, that we only have forty minutes. He says, "No problem. Last name Carey, right?" I feel a little embarrassed that he knows my voice. I say politely as I can, "That's right. Thanks so much."

Sarah and I meet by the trophy case and walk out to the parking lot together. Leigh is already waiting for us in her mom's car.

"Cool," I say, getting into the backseat.

"Yeah, Leigh," Sarah says and shuts the door. "How'd you get out here so fast?"

"I left physics early."

"You must have Mr. Holbrook," Sarah says. "I have him first period, and I'm always late. He doesn't care."

"Well, we can't be late coming back from lunch," I tell

Leigh. "We have geometry fourth. Mrs. Schneider."

Leigh nods and starts driving. "Want some music?"

"Yeah, baby," Sarah says and starts turning the dial.

We're just about to leave the lot when we hear a horn blaring behind us. We all turn to see Trey hanging halfway out the window of his new black Firebird, his white jersey waving. We take a right and a quick left onto Cliff Drive, the road that Hardscrabble Country Club is on, and Trey follows us, with his shiny chrome rims, his big tires, his tail fin high in the air.

"God, what a tacky car," I say.

"It's not that bad," Sarah says. "I kind of like it."

"I'd rather be in this one," I say. "Right, Leigh?"

Leigh turns back and smiles at me, then looks ahead, speeding up a little. Cliff Drive is a long, windy road lined with expensive houses with long driveways. It's hard to see the houses from the road, but Leigh keeps glancing back and forth, trying to see something. Sarah rolls down her window and climbs halfway out, the purple streaks in her dark hair blowing, and yells "woo" over to Trey like she's at a concert.

"Good Lord," I say and pull on her to get back in. "Be careful."

"Hey," she says. "Relax."

As we round the corner coming up to the club, I turn around and see Trey taking the curve too fast. His car swings off the road, jackknifes, then goes into a ditch, only his stupid tail fin showing. Sarah sees it, too, and laughs.

"What a moron!" I say.

"What is it?" asks Leigh, and Sarah tells her what she missed.

Leigh slows down and takes the exit for Hardscrabble.

She circles the lot, hesitating. "Should we go back?"

"No, he's fine," I say. "He's wrecked there twice before."

"Yeah, don't worry about little Trey, Leigh baby," Sarah says. "Try to park up front."

"Yeah," I say. "Time is of the essence." This is a phrase my mother uses when I'm running late, which is almost always.

We rush into the country club and walk through the bar, and Sarah and I grab nuts and mints from little bowls set around on small marble tables. In the dining room, we sit by a window, so we have a good view of the golf course. Sarah tells Leigh about how I almost killed her with a 7 iron. She always tells that story whenever she gets the chance.

A waiter comes up to us with menus, but I tell him we already ordered by phone, and he smiles and fills our water glasses and takes our drink order. I get a Coke like always, and Sarah gets a virgin strawberry daiquiri, and Leigh orders iced tea.

Leigh leans over and says in a hushed voice, "Is everyone that works here black?"

I shrug. "I guess."

"I think I've seen a few white ones before," Sarah says, then waves her hand and gets a different waiter to bring us crackers and bread and butter.

"This is really nice," Leigh says. "Thanks for bringing me here."

"Thanks for driving us here," Sarah says, buttering a cracker.

The waiter returns with our sandwiches on a big round tray he carries with one hand above his shoulder, and another waiter follows him, like he's the other waiter's waiter, carrying our drinks.

"Cool," I say. "We still have twenty-seven minutes."

On the side of Leigh's plate are silver cups with mayonnaise and mustard, and she spreads both on each layer of the four triangles of her sandwich. Sarah and I dig into our French dips and have a silver cup of ketchup between us for our fries.

"This is way better than the school cafeteria," Leigh says.

"Chandler and I," says Sarah, "have never eaten there. We've successfully gotten a ride every day for three months. And in just four more months, we won't have to. I'm sixteen in March."

"When are you sixteen, Chandler?" Leigh says.

I take a drink of my Coke. "Not until next September."

"God," Leigh says. "I'm almost a year older."

"Chandler's got a bad birthday," Sarah explains, holding her virgin daiquiri like it's real. "If she were just one month younger, she could play sixteen-and-under tennis for an extra year." Sarah waves her drink around. "So Leigh, what's up with your mom?"

Leigh takes a bite of her sandwich, then a drink of her iced tea. "What do you mean?"

I eat a fry and Leigh doesn't say anything, so I say, "Nothing's up with her. She just calls in sick a lot."

"She hates working," Leigh says.

"Man, I don't blame her." Sarah raises her glass and says, "To not ever having to work."

Leigh smiles, and I smile.

"Let's get out of here," I say. "Time is of the essence."

I raise my hand for the waiter, and he brings over our ticket, and I sign my father's name with a short yellow pencil, *Ben L. Carey #379.*

We have about five minutes before the bell rings. What takes the most time is finding a parking place in the school lot. But Leigh tells us not to worry about it and that if we're late getting back, she'll drop us off by the door.

Leigh turns on the radio and switches the dial around and stops on a commercial that we all know by heart, and we say together in a deep, dopey voice, "C&H Tire. 8701 Rogers. Where we do it just for you."

Leigh takes a right onto Cliff Drive, and we only go about ten yards because there's so much traffic. It normally gets a little backed up every day with kids rushing from McDonald's or Wendy's, but this is way worse than usual.

Sarah's in the backseat this time, and she yells up, "What the hell?"

Leigh is quiet, concentrating, moving the car slowly.

"I can't tell," I say. I roll down the window and lean out as far as I can. In the distance, I can see a fire truck and blue police lights. A cop is waving cars around.

Sarah leans up, too, and tries to get a look. "Is that all for Trey?" she says.

"It has to be," Leigh says.

We creep forward, and as we approach the curve, I see Trey's black Firebird still tipped down into the ditch. His shiny chrome rims, his big tires, his tail fin.

"That looks pretty bad," Leigh says.

I feel relieved when I see Trey standing there by a cop. He looks fine. The back of his white jersey is clean around the number and not torn or anything. The cop is probably talking to him about the big away game tonight in Pine Bluff, which is pretty far from Fort Smith, about four hours. I think the football team is supposed to leave right after lunch. Trey's probably worried about missing the bus. "Thank God," I say. "He's okay. He's right there."

Sarah is still leaning up over the seat, but she doesn't say anything.

"That's not him," Leigh says. "That's someone else. Trey's #48."

"She's right," Sarah says.

Leigh inches the car forward, then the policeman directing traffic makes us stop, and we're right next to Trey's car. Leigh shifts into park, and we all look. The front end is crumpled by at least three feet against the side of the ditch. Firemen are working to cut Trey out. The door is open, but his body is wrapped around the steering wheel. His head stuffed between the dash and the windshield. There is blood on his jersey and on his head and in the cracks of the glass.

I look away and notice that people are starting to drive around us and that we're the ones who are holding things up. The policeman knocks on the back of our car and startles us, tells us to get moving. Leigh puts the car in drive, and we proceed.

Nobody says anything. Maybe we don't know what to say, or what to think. I look at one of the fancy houses and think that I like my house better. And I like Sarah's house even better than mine. She lives in this long sprawling one on the other side of Hardscrabble, on the back nine of the golf course. Sometimes, when I spend the night over there, we'll sneak out and meet guys.

One night Trey met us there with another football player. I was the one who was supposed to be with Trey, but we still had the same problem talking to each other. We lay down on a green, the short grass more perfect than carpet, and looked at the stars. We never kissed, but he put his arm around me, and his other hand rubbed on my shoulder and on my elbow and on my wrist and on my palm and on each finger. He was the first boy to ever touch me like that, and I never even kissed him.

Traffic is moving almost back to normal. The second lunch has already started, and we see kids breeze by the other way, not knowing what's ahead.

Leigh turns off the radio. Sarah starts crying. Leigh looks over to me, and I look back to her, then put my hand over my eyes. Sarah's breathing is loud and erratic. Leigh turns into the lot.

"You can go ahead and park," I say.

"No, I'll drop you off," she says. "I want to."

She pulls up to the entrance of the school, and I wipe my eyes.

"You sure?" I ask. "We'll wait and walk in with you."

"No, go ahead," she says.

I open my door and get out, then pull the seat forward for Sarah. I grip her arm and steady her until she's standing. I start to thank Leigh for the ride but stop myself. I want to tell her that I'm sorry, that we should've gone back, I should've let her go back, but I don't say anything, just shut the door and watch her drive off, all by herself, looking for a place to park.

Sarah and I walk into the school, and I'm wondering how long it will take to forget this walk. It seems too quiet. There should be a commotion in the halls. Others saw what we saw, but classes have already started, and we are going to be late.

CAVITY STAR
Jamie Kornegay

The boy Gum was built like a squat torpedo. No neck or
waist, and he walked into the dentist's nook encumbered,
like he was carrying something wrong in his britches. Doc
suspected it of all four-year-olds.

"I'm gawna get me a pwize!" Gum announced, hands
on hips. "Weir's dat toy baw-ux?"

"Get on back up front with your mamma," said Doc,
unamused by the interruption. He was working on a patient in an orange jumpsuit, a convict from county lock-up
named Wade Sommers. The sheriff was always sending
Wade over to the office with a busted tooth from gnawing
on his cell bars.

"I wawunt my pwize!"

"You don't get no prize," Doc replied. "Little boys with
cavities don't get prizes."

Gum stopped to consider this. "I ... wawunt ... my ...
PWIZE!!!"

"Sashu luwil boowa," said Wade.

"What?" said Doc, removing his latex fingers from
Wade's mouth and dabbing saliva on the patient's paper bib.

"I says, ain't he a sassy li'l booger. Why don't—"

"I WAWUNT MY PWIZE!" the kid shrieked, so loud it got into the men's pits.

"Damn, son," said Wade. "Doc, why don't you give that scooter his prize and get his scrawny li'l ass outta here?"

"Wade, there's nothing I'd like better at this moment." Doc looked on the boy with spite—his clogged nose and sassy mouth stained fluoride red. He leaned over and whispered to Wade. "Dorothy forgot to order the toy prizes from the reseller up in Memphis."

"Don't seem right," Wade replied. "To scrape and pull at a little feller's tooth all mornin and not give him his prize. Seems as long as you been workin teeth, Doc, you'd be a little more tender."

"Tell you what," said Doc, reaching into his pocket for some change. He handed the coins to Gum. "Why don't you run up the corner to Mr. Jiffy and buy you a tater log?"

The boy knocked the money out of Doc's hand and howled something indecipherable. No negative or affirmative, just a piercing screech that startled both men.

"There's something bad wrong here," Doc said, then stepped out to the lobby to fetch the boy's mamma. There was no one around, just strewn magazines and wrappers from the charity peppermint box. The boy continued screaming in the back.

"Hush that racket up before I go back yonder and get a switch off that dogwood!" Doc called as he returned to the examination room. The boy had fallen to the floor and was wallowing on the linoleum. He kicked and wailed and rolled beneath the reclining dentist chair. A tray of utensils toppled over and clattered impressively.

Wade was nervous. The bright light wrapped in tin foil

scalded his eyes.

"Dorothy!" Doc cried. "Where's this boy's mamma?" Dorothy did not reply. She was out back smoking a cigarette.

Gum screamed and floundered around the small office. He knocked over a big plaster molar and started stirring up soil in a potted plant in the corner.

"Get out of there, you little gremlin!" cried Doc, snatching up Gum. He was a heavy kid, and no fool. He threw his arms straight up and slipped out of the Doc's grasp like a slick catfish.

"Doc! You'll throw your back out monkeyin wit that kid," hollered Wade. "I don't see why ya don't just hook him up to the gas."

"Nitrous oxide? He's too young for that. It's liable to retard his little brain."

"My daddy used to give me ether when I was his age."

Doc frowned as Gum began bawling and rubbing the crotch of his corduroys.

Wade stopped and stared. "It ain't wise to upset a convict, boy."

Gum stood up. With his face toward the corner, he pouted to the plant. "I wawunt my pwize."

"Hell, he's already half retard it seems," said Wade.

Gum looked suspicious, all hunched up in the corner and rocking his hips. "Hey, son," Doc called. "What's that you're doing over there?"

The boy turned his old sour dough head around. The words skipped off his fat lips. "Tee-teein!"

Doc growled and jerked the youngster back, then examined the plant. It looked a little damp.

"What the hell's the meaning of coming in here acting

like this?" Doc demanded. "Where's your mamma?"

Gum cocked his little arm back as if to strike the Doc. "I wawunt my pwize, cuckoo bwain!" The boy threw a trial-size tube of toothpaste that hit Doc square in the groin.

"Strap him down and turn that gas on!" urged Wade. "They ain't a gas on the planet that'd mess up that li'l rascal any worse than he already is."

The boy reached into his pants to begin again, but Doc grabbed him by the shoulders and shook the small, jiggling menace. "All right, then. Hop up, Wade. We're gonna strap this little one down and put him to sleep til his mamma gets back."

Wade jumped up, and Doc hoisted the squirming boy into the dentist chair. He pulled the face mask from the sea green tank and adjusted the strap so that it would fit around the boy's fruit bowl head, then clamped it over his whooping mouth.

Just then the boy stopped his wiggling and looked teary-eyed at Doc and the convict. His pudgy bottom lip quivered inside the rubber mask, and he cocked his head like a puppy. His eyes welled up, red like a swollen gum-line.

"I jes wawunt my pwize," said the sad muffled voice.

Doc pursed his lips and felt ashamed. Wade felt a burn behind his eyeball and a twitch in his nose. But convicts don't cry.

"Here go li'l, man," Wade spoke up. He peeled a tiny gold-star sticker off the lapel of his orange jumpsuit. "I got this for good behavior over the weekend. I got a collection of 'em up on my wall, but I want you to have this one."

Wade pasted the gold star on the collar of Gum's Izod. The boy gave a sad clown smile and looked coy. "But I wawunt a toy."

Doc raised up. "Tell you what. I got a sling-shot that Old Mr. Walker brought in here last week."

Doc pilfered through a drawer and retrieved the sling-shot.

"It's fine quality. Mind you don't put your eye out."

The boy flipped off the mask, snatched the sling-shot and leaped from the chair. He made a rude noise with his mouth and stuck his butt in the air before he bolted, his shoes squeaking down the hall. The waiting room door slammed shut, knocking a picture of a tooth cross-section off the wall in the examination room.

"I ought not take no more kids," Doc said.

FLOATING
Sidney Thompson

Larry Havard had spent almost every free weekend of his life hunting in the South Mississippi woods of his home county, but for almost a month now, at age thirty-six, he hadn't had the heart to kill one thing. Not after his house caught fire and he lost the best bird dogs he'd ever owned or heard of, two full-blooded retrievers, to smoke inhalation.

Yesterday he'd even flinched at his uncle Posey's hog killing. He'd actually felt sorry for the hog when his aging uncle kept losing his aim—taking him four tries to finally hit the brain and put the squealing thing down on the trailer floor.

His poor suffering bird dogs, King-Size and Copperhead, was the only thought his mind could muster. And that scared Larry. Not since perhaps his seventh birthday, when the first blast of his new single-shot 12 gauge thrust the stock under his arm and the hammer snagged his cheek, had he sympathized with any dying creature. He could still clean meat and knife it up, but he just couldn't bring himself to kill.

That's why he cut out of work early today to go to the

shelter. Maybe he'd luck up on a couple of healthy lab pups or maybe a beagle bitch primed for coon.

But all Larry found on either side of the kennel walkway was what the dog catcher had promised. Only nippers, lungers, and broken dogs with mange or missing parts. A few yard dogs in the bunch, sure, but not one up-and-comer. Not one that was the least bit alert or even tame. Every hunter he knew penned their dogs up and starved them to keep them wild and forever ready but would eventually run them to death or lose them in the woods. Larry had been the same way until he'd discovered that the more he tamed King-Size and Copperhead with rewards, the longer they'd run and they'd always come back. A pooch might not be smarter than a human, but Larry swore it wasn't dumber.

When he reached the last of the cages and spotted a little wavy-haired something-or-other backed in a corner, he lowered to his boot heels and wiggled a finger through the chain link. He expected the dog to raise its nose to check him out, at least its black, stunned eyes to blink. He'd never suspected his finger would scare it and make it shake. And even after he'd drawn back his hand, the dog, an old white poodle with a yellow face, continued to tremble, without once losing its stare, and that reminded Larry of yesterday's hog. A two-hundred pounder, solid black except for the white cloud mark across its back. It too, while staring at Larry, had begun to shake—and just when the kettle water had begun to boil, as if the hog understood. Larry remembered looking away then, his eyes following the rising steam, watching it merge with the smoke from the driftwood fire and pass downwind, above the cow pasture, into a halo of buzzards.

The weepy sorrow in the poodle's eyes made him want to reach out. Not since he was a boy had he had a dog just for petting. But such a notion aggravated him and he shot up to leave. He hadn't come there to pick out a toy. He was full of mud. What in the world was he thinking?

The custodian who'd been sanitizing empty cages at the far end of the kennel was now plodding in waders in Larry's direction.

"Case you're wanting that poodle there, it's got heartworms," the custodian told him. "Man brung him in just awhile ago to be put down."

Larry shrugged. "Oh, well," he said, then brushed on past.

But minutes later panic lit into him as if he'd received again the fire department's call. With his truck still running, he hurried back inside, afraid the custodian had already gassed the poor thing. And when he neared the cage, fear swept fresh the sight of his huddled blackened dogs. But this, he realized, was a different day. He found the little old cryface exactly where he'd left him—though completely still now. Not quite serene just yet but not any more scared either. Almost waiting.

Seeing as the dog's doom was a foregone conclusion, Larry figured he ought to be the one to put it down. And by being the one, maybe he'd conquer his worrisome death tic once and for all.

"Yeah," he said, and he snatched the dog from its cage.

Larry drove slower than usual on his way home. He even felt comfortable enough to drape his arm across the seat. His wife had moved out nine months ago and gotten the divorce finalized, so it felt good to look over and see a passenger looking back at him. The poodle was old but didn't look that old, not to be dying yet, but here it was and he was glad. King-Size and Copperhead had always wanted to ride together in the back to lick the wind and bark at passing dogs. He also usually kept his stereo blaring Cream or Skynyrd, but this time he turned it down.

At home, he helped the poodle to the ground and watched to make sure it didn't wander into the yard, where the scorched lumber was still strewn, and step on a nail. Then once it lowered its leg from an impressive 70-degree hike, Larry picked the old stud-boy up and carried him inside.

The poodle sniffed in circles across the kitchen floor, while Larry wiped his mustache out of the corners of his mouth. He reached under the sink and pulled out the retrievers' water bowl and scrubbed away the waves of smoke with his hands and a bar of soap. He rinsed it, and then dried it with a paper towel, and then filled it up with cold water. He set the bowl down and stepped back to the refrigerator, and the poodle hesitated over and lapped like frogs leaping from a bank. That's what it sounded like to Larry, anyway.

Larry grinned at the beard of water dripping from the dog's chin. "You weren't thirsty, were you, boy? And I bet you ain't hungry either, huh?" He opened the freezer to see what he could cook special enough for a last meal.

There was plenty left over from his hunting days to choose from, but the pursuit ended when he found a front-quarter shoulder of deer meat. He wouldn't have wanted anything else if it were his time coming.

So while the deer-meat T-bone thawed in a sink of hot water, Larry went through the house cutting the lights on in every room so that he could re-examine the past month's work and consider what remained ahead of him. After he'd gutted the house of all its wood paneling, carpeting and melted ceiling tiles and linoleum, replaced the necessary studs, rafters and floorboards, and had painted Kilz over all smoke-damaged wood, he rewired the house, insulated it and put in new windows, then did for himself what he did nearly every day at work for others. He hung the sheetrock, which he'd finished nailing up only last night. And tomorrow he'd begin the floating, his specialty.

The process involved hiding all uncomely aspects of the sheetrock beneath layers of tape and mud, so that what remained for the painter were level lines from corner to every corner, even if the house wasn't square. He didn't exactly understand the name. All he could figure was that the person who'd come up with it must have noticed, like he had, that if you sink yourself to the bottom of Brushy Creek, you'll see there's enough silt and sand in the water to make whatever and whoever floating above appear too vague to be visible.

Sometimes people in the community would try hanging their own sheetrock, but nobody but a floater had better float it. Not unless they didn't mind the rows of nail heads showing through on the walls like shirt buttons. But if they wanted their rooms to appear seamless and whole, as though one single wall folded into a box, or if they needed enough mud troweled at the top and bottom to make a bowed wall appear plumb, then Larry was the man. And the stage of floating he liked best—even more than troweling the sheetrock mud over a nasty gash—was gently sanding the sheetrock, once it had dried, to a smooth finish with his sandstone, the size of a brick, and watching fine white dust cloud up under the brushing of his stone and fall like snow, and there'd be banks of it everywhere, along every wall. Real snow had fallen in George County only a few times in his life, but even on those occasions it never completely covered up anything.

Most of what had been salvaged from the fire and not ruined by the smoke and water was being stored in a friend's vacant barn, so the only furniture in the house consisted of what his cousin, the supply sergeant at the National Guard Armory, had loaned him: a field table and a cot, both set up out of the way of the work, in the kitchen. He didn't believe he was ready yet to sleep in the bedroom anyway. He still found himself shaking his head and gazing in dismay at the blackened pine floor where his bed had been. Where he'd flipped back the mattress and box spring and discovered his dogs still trying side-by-side, it seemed, to hide from the fire. He'd lifted their limp heads, touched their pallid tongues, then with the edge of his boot, had scraped their feces to the wall.

After the divorce, he'd started letting his dogs live inside, and his folks were afraid he was losing his mind. His momma had even sent for the preacher to visit him. But he was merely protecting his remaining assets, Larry had done his best to explain, to his family and to the preacher. But to his buddies, cousins included, who feared those prize bird dogs would become spoiled, he told another story: just trying to run the smell of the ex-wife clean from the house.

Larry turned to cut off the light in the bedroom and spotted little cryface peeking at him from around the corner in the hallway. "Yeah, you're probably right," he smiled. He followed the pooch into the kitchen, and sure enough the boy's T-bone was ready for the oven. And while the shoulder meat baked, he fried up a couple of hot sausage links and boiled a pot of rice for himself. Every once in a while he'd pop a beer and sit down at the table and eye the poodle, who'd hopped on the cot and was making himself right at home. He liked looking at the dog sometimes, but sometimes he didn't.

His own food was ready before the dog's, so he set it aside under cover. When the T-bone had cooled some, he cut it up and served it on the floor where he'd made a clean spot in the dust.

"Enjoy, little thing," he said, and the boy lost all shyness, as if this were his first meeting with the taste of deer. And when he'd devoured the shoulder meat, Larry tossed him the bone. He was proud of himself for giving this dog a last-minute friendly place. He'd done a good deed, his first in a long time that no one could take from him.

When Larry finished eating, he put his dishes in the sink and rummaged in the cupboard until he'd found the cane syrup. Then he went to his truck for his .45 and sat back down at the table. The boy was still having his way on the deer bone, and Larry wasn't about to take it away. When the boy decided he was done with it, then that would be the time. And until that moment, Larry would down as many beers as the dog gave him time to. Which happened to be three.

The bone dropped from between his paws as the dog stood up and stretched his hind legs. Then he walked on to the water bowl.

Larry reached into his pocket for his face rag. "Come here, boy," he said and kissed the air, and the poodle trotted over. He picked him up and set him on his lap, then wiped the boy's chin with the rag. "Well," he said, stroking the dog, "I'm sorry."

He held him high in the crook of his arm and rose to his feet, tucking the .45 into his beltline. Once he'd grabbed the syrup can, the empty house echoed with his footsteps.

He stopped out back by the toolshed for his spade and his flashlight before crossing through the yard and entering the unfenced woods, which gently sloped downward from his lot a quarter of a mile. And where it leveled was a place among the clustered pine that a full moon overhead could not penetrate. Where he'd seen last year from the nearby spring, with the aid of his cousin's night-vision goggles, two deer mating. Where almost a month ago he'd dug a hole large enough in which to lay King-Size and Copperhead chest to chest. Where all that could smother a soul was pure pine.

Larry knelt beside the washed-out mound of the grave, and on a throw of needles he began freeing himself—first of the flashlight, then the shovel, and when the syrup can clanked against the two, the poodle tensed up and locked his forelegs, and his claws dug into Larry's neck as though the dog had every intention of roosting there.

"This'll be painless, boy," he said, trying to calm the rigid dog, petting the whole length of him. "Quick and sweet," he said, "I promise." He was thinking of the hog he should've (and could've) killed himself with one shot, but he'd declined to take his uncle's rifle, saying a man ought to shoot his own.

Larry pulled the poodle to his chest and cradled him as he eased himself to the ground on folded legs. And once he'd begun again to stroke the dog and talk to him, the dog started to relax in his lap. And with the same ease, he slipped the .45 revolver from his waistband and used its sight to pry the lid off the syrup can. Before the fire, he'd gotten in the habit of letting the retrievers lick the drippings off the can, and the poodle, craning his bobbing nose to investigate, seemed no less interested.

The hunter was an instrument of mercy, and that was what he always needed to remember. He was helping the poor, dumb animals to survive the worst possible fate. That being shot was ever better than slowly losing breath in the heat of fire. If done without notice and with care.

Larry dipped the nose of the barrel into the syrup and offered it to him, and the dog hesitantly swiped it with the tip of his tongue. "It's okay," he said, "have all you want. That's good stuff," he said, and the dog agreed, returning for more. And when the boy's fast tongue had cleaned the barrel, Larry dipped it again. This time, though, he didn't completely bring it to the dog but held it a half foot from him, and as soon as the dog had begun to lick it, he pulled it slowly away from him another half foot, so that the boy was now totally uprooted from Larry's lap.

When the poodle started nibbling the barrel, Larry took the gun away once more and dipped it down to the cylinder. The dog wagged his tail, appearing youthful and unmasked in the amber light. Then rolling onto his back, the dog stretched his paws to hold onto the dripping gun himself. The dog was really lapping in the cane. And Larry, panting, cocked his head back and, hallelujah, pulled the trigger.

That wasn't too bad. He was fine. Nothing to it, he told himself. He rose to his feet and began shoveling the red clay. He was sure he could hunt again now and was grateful to the boy and said so as he lowered him down.

Maybe the shelter would have something special for him tomorrow too, he thought. Maybe something he could feed more than once. Something he could name, and a proud name he could holler. And on his way back to the house, he found himself smiling at the good names he could choose from. Moocher, Kaiser, Biscuit, and Red-Eye, and there'd come a day, he was sure, that a dog could rightfully be tagged Larry. Larry and Larry.

Life, he could tell, would be different for him now. The way it used to be. He dropped by the toolshed, then kicked off his boots at the back door and slung off his jacket. Yeah, he thought, setting the syrup and the .45 in the kitchen sink, old Larry was back. Only new and improved.

He gazed at his cot as he unbuttoned his shirt. Without blinking he continued to undress, to remove his undershirt, and then he paused to follow, with the tips of his fingers, the smooth, thin line that diagonally crossed his obliterated left nipple. He wasn't remembering the day a .22 cartridge had grazed there, nor because of the incident his now-former hunting buddy. Rather, he was trying to recall the evenings when he'd sighted the deer that he could not, in his own way, call his own. He knew there were two, a yearling and then a week later a buck. One nuzzling the fallen leaves for acorns and the other turning its four points to the wind. One emerging into open field and one already there. He could remember that much. What he had trouble recalling was himself. How he must have appeared to them once he'd stepped from hiding with his hat clutched at his side. Which lucky flannel shirt had he worn? How would he know never to wear it again?

He'd just about decided to forget the matter though and go take his bath when he heard someone pulling up the gravel drive. He stopped stroking his scar, then smiled at his cousin's knack of perfect timing. Somehow Stringer's blood always knew where to lead him, as it had in Desert Storm, and such as here, on this big night, probably to spotlight deer in the back woods. But when Larry looked out the kitchen window and saw a car instead of a truck, he put his shirt back on and, leaving it unbuttoned, went to the front door with his .45.

When he stepped outside and found a woman seated alone in a four-door, an Accord, Larry tucked his .45 away and leaned against a porch post. He watched the woman, maybe late twenties, unbuckle herself and then do a little this and a little that, and then she finally opened her door and asked if he were Larry Havard.

"Well," he said, "now that depends largely on who you are."

She shut the door, and as she approached the porch, Larry admired the nice tossed-up deal with her hair, and her figure wasn't too bad either. Her shoes looking top dollar.

"I was told at the animal shelter that you adopted a poodle today—a white poodle, about eight years old. Is that right?" she asked. "Are you that Larry Havard? This is 2203 Cooks Corner Road, isn't it?"

Larry nodded his head, or thought he did. "And who might you be?" he asked.

"I'm the owner," she said. "Puddles—that's the poodle's name—that's my dog."

"Do what?" he said.

"They told me at the shelter that you saved his life." She stepped closer, her eyes dark like his ex-wife's but bigger, more white to see, and she clasped Larry's hand inside both of hers. "Believe me," she said, holding his hand more than shaking it, "I'd never dump anything of mine in a place like that, especially if it had heartworms. I've got a neighbor, you see, who plainly detests all newcomers and says so to your face, so I know he's the one that dropped Puddles off. The people at the shelter described him to a tee. So I'm here to take my dog home now, if you don't mind, please sir. I'll pay you for your trouble, of course."

Larry drew away his hand, and almost breathless he fell back against the post and folded his arms. "You're saying your dog didn't have heartworms, or that he did?"

She smirked. "That dog's the picture of health, you kidding me? He could be old for another ten years. Easy." She forked a hand through her hair, giving it a fresh toss, then explained how Puddles spotted a possum in a tree one night and barked an hour straight. And how twice the dog had gotten off his chain and torn into the neighbor's cheap, thin trash-bags. "He ought to buy a can," she said, "like everybody else. Those are the reasons he wanted my dog destroyed. Can you imagine?" Her face slacked, then startling Larry she suddenly clapped her hands together and grinned. "So where's my Puddles at?" she asked. "Where's my little baby?"

Larry cleared his throat. "Well, ma'am," he said and cleared his throat again. "I did pick your Puddles up and bring him home with me, yes ma'am, I did. And I fed him good too, real good, but I'm sorry, I'm terribly sorry, lady." Larry shrugged and had to turn away from her horror, and he found himself remembering his own and staring into the shadows at the scorched lumber pile. "I had no idea the thing was a little Houdini," he said. He hooked a thumb over his shoulder. "I chained him out back but he got loose, just about an hour ago."

He glanced to see how she was taking it, and she was taking it better than he'd hoped. Almost as if she believed he was lying and the dog was still chained up. "I went looking for him," he told her. "Went up this road a dozen times, and all the roads around, but I couldn't find him." She was shaking her head, and he said, "I'm sorry. I just gave up."

"He couldn't be far, though," she said and bolted to her car. He watched her reach dashward, to the glove compartment, and hop out with a beaming flashlight. "With these woods you have around here, you wouldn't find him on a road. He doesn't like roads. But woods? That poodle lives to chase squirrels." She whipped around and plowed full-steam through the side yard, heading toward his neighbor's woods.

"Hold up," he called, but she was on course, and who was he to stop her? He had to go put on his boots and grab his jacket. But by the time he'd done all that and run back out, she was only a slight glow sweeping west.

Once he'd ducked through the barbed wire, he followed a winding trail more memorized than beaten. And when the trail began instead to draw him away from her, he thrashed through the trees, following the mournful beacon of her dog's name.

And then above him on higher land he spotted a streak of light. "Miss?" he said, the briars popping at his jeans, and the light turned and slanted upon the ground and caught him in the eyes.

"Puddles? Puddles, is that you?" she asked.

He bowed his head from the glare and flagged her with his hand. The light then dropped to an oval at her feet and was switched off. But he could see her still, standing above him, her silhouette in the starlight, her shoulders lifting and lowering, and that amazed Larry. He'd never known until this moment that a person from twenty or so yards away could be observed breathing with only the naked eye. A buck, sure, and any rabbit, but a human? A woman? He wouldn't have guessed.

"Are you coming?" she asked.

"Yeah," he said, pushing on, "I'm coming."

"I would've gotten to your house sooner," she said, "but I didn't know how to find it and your phone's not listed."

"I don't have one," he said, continuing his climb. "Not at home, only at my shop. In town I run my own sheetrocking business."

"And I got lost," she said.

When he reached her, she was sitting on an uprooted hickory.

"My house about burnt to the ground last month because of a faulty breaker," he told her, and when she continued to keep her face tipped down, he stepped toward the hickory and pulled a clod of dirt from the root of a root and broke it up. "Also, I come to find out the joker who built the house put in the wrong grade of wire, so I ended up losing my two dogs. Two golden retrievers."

She raised her head in his direction but not to look at him, now sitting on the trunk by the roots. "And though one was bigger," he said, "and the other more red and was a girl, you could tell it they were twins. That's why I was at the pound in the first place today—to find me another hunting dog or two. But then I some way or another fell for your poodle dog." He chuckled. "But what do you think," he asked, and she looked at him, "you think your dog, with a little training, could've made a good squirrel dog?"

She smiled. "He loved to chase squirrels."

He nodded, until she turned away and wiped the corners of her eyes with her knuckles. "So where are you from?" he asked.

"Memphis," she said.

"Memphis!" He whistled. "What in the world brought you all the way down here?"

He watched her trace the crisscrossing pattern of the bark with her fingertips. Then she stopped and began to pick at the trunk's bark with her fingernails. He was starting to think she didn't hear him or had forgotten to speak when she said she was teaching at the high school.

"But ain't they got schools up north?" he asked. "I mean, why God's country?"

"My ex-husband doesn't live in God's country," she said.

"I see," said Larry. "I understand."

She flicked her nails together and stood up, brushing her hand against her pants. "So where do we go from here?" She switched on her light.

Thinking they ought to cover the entire wooded radius, he pointed to the southeast, back toward his own property, and led the way. He'd whistle and snap his fingers, and then they'd alternate and he'd be the one calling the boy's name. Nearly every twenty feet they'd both stop and listen for Puddles bounding through the brush or for a distant bark. Sometimes Larry would have to remind himself not to expect too much.

When they reached the spring and heard again the dogless night, Larry knelt and scooped water into his mouth.

"Have a drink," he told her. "It's clean." But she remained standing, scanning the woods.

"I'm not trying to be smart or tell you what to do," she said. "I'm just curious. I've always wondered why people hunt. Why really?"

Larry wiped his mouth on his jacket sleeve. "I can only speak for myself," he said.

"That's fine," she said, casting her light over him as he rose to his feet.

"No mystery, I don't think," he said. "To eat. But I ain't been eating lately."

Her light stuttered and she shook it, and it burned a little brighter. "But how do you do it?" she asked. "How do you shoot one animal and then pet on another that's not that much different?"

He shrugged. "I don't know. I been wrestling with that lately, and honestly I can't figure out how I done that."

She smiled. "I'm really surprised somebody like you would pick out a dog with heartworms to have as a pet. With the trouble and expense already of rebuilding your house?" She shook her head and he began to nod. "And heartworm treatment is expensive. That was amazingly kind of you, you know that?"

But Larry was shocked that she would expect him to pay for such treatment. He didn't think holes in the heart should be floated.

She bent down to the spring. "Very generous," she said. She smelled her hand that she had dipped into the water. Then she dipped again and this time she drank, and Larry pulled out his face rag and she took it and dried her hand. "Let's go that way," she said, darting light over stomped needles and leaves of a trail heading northward. There was a more eastward trail, less beaten, he could've tried steering her to, but he didn't. He was sure she was tracking.

She bellowed the boy's name and forged ahead, but Larry was silent now, eaten up with missing all three dogs, and wondering if he was doing right.

When she entered the pine grove, he watched her slow, then tip her light to the red churned earth and pat her feet in the soil. She turned with a look of question and sorrow.

"My dogs," he said, and she groaned.

"I'm sorry." She stepped back and let the light linger over the small section of darker earth at the tail end of the grave. "It happened a month ago, you said?"

"Yeah, just a month ago."

She continued to stare at the grave, or study it, and then she looked up and he wondered if she were studying him.

"A grave'll stay fresh a long time in this climate. You'll get used to it." He smiled, to ease her some, but she dropped her head down and he couldn't tell if she were about to cry or pray.

"I wouldn't worry too much about little Puddles," he said. "Somebody could've found him by now and be taking good care of him. Or he might come strolling up any minute. Little Puddles right now could be having himself a big old ball filling up on squirrel meat," he said, and waited for her to laugh. When she didn't, he stepped up beside her.

"I think we've searched enough for tonight," she said, nodding, but still not looking at him. "I can try again to-morrow." She beamed light on the trees around them. "Where's the way out of here?"

Larry set his hands on his hips. "I wish I could've done more for you, though."

She shook her head, and then he noticed her whole

body was shaking. "I'm tired," she said, her voice shaking. "I want to go home."

"Okay, sure, of course," he said. He walked around Puddles' grave, but only after he'd squeezed through pines to leave the grove did he hear her make any move to follow. He imagined her hanging back, terrified, and suffocating her cry so he wouldn't hear it. He thought of how the caulking around his tub still wept soot.

He watched her dim light flicker at the ground, then felt it flicker on his face. "I must look like some country demon, huh?"

"Oh, no," she said. "You don't."

"If I could back up time and choose the way I could have it, it wouldn't even be a choice. I might be wrong, but when it comes to finding out tragedy, I'll take not finding over finding any day. The biggest lie of a hope over a fact any day." He flung open his arms. "King-Size and Copperhead are actually alive and licking the face of my worst enemy? Well, good for them. See what I mean? Maybe in the big scheme of things it was good that your neighbor lied. You might not have Puddles, somebody else might have Puddles, but who knows, what if the Lord meant for us to meet this way and go out some time, you know? That's all I'm saying."

She panted, then said, "Hmmm." Or maybe she was clearing her throat to speak. He waited, and when nothing else came, Larry turned around and hiked the rest of the way out of the woods. He stopped again, on the open slope of his backyard, so he could see her under the clear sky.

"There's one more thing we can do tonight if you're up to it," he said.

She shook her head and walked past him.

"I got some squirrel meat in the freezer I could fry up right quick," he said, following her. "I was thinking maybe Puddles might smell it and come a running." He snickered. "We could at least get our strength back. The meat's got to be ate, and I bet you never ate squirrel before. You ought to try it before there ain't none. It's the last thing I ever kill to eat, I swear to you. Killing's out of my system for good. We'll make it a feast in our little fellow's honor. What do you say?"

But she walked on, heading around the house faster than he could follow, and when she reached her car, she said nothing. She slammed her door and locked it and started the engine and backed away in a whip and sped off.

Smelling the dust that the Accord had turned up from the drive, he was reminded of the day his ex-wife had made her exit, under similar circumstances, after he'd given just as many assurances. Maybe he could never really talk to anyone. And then for a reason that seemed to him otherworldly, he remembered the moment he'd unleashed King-Size and Copperhead into the house. How they had confronted, in the oven door, their own reflections. How, in their delightful confusion, the dogs had growled and wagged their tails at once.

He smiled at the memory, and feeling almost drunk from the notion that his dogs had fetched that smile themselves, he lolled his head back and stared at the unfinished ceiling of night, with all its irregular clouds and clusters, and he wished he could strip off his shirt and swim into the sky, to be unseen and forgotten forever.

THE COOL OF THE DAY
Silas House

On Fridays Rita makes Adam undress on the back porch. She cleans the house extra-good on that day, and says she doesn't want him packing in coal dust. Every Friday when he gets home she is always sitting there on the second step, usually peeling potatoes or breaking beans or doing something in the business of getting supper started. He wonders why she always sits on the step even though the back porch is crowded with enough chairs to seat a church meeting, but he has never asked her about it.

In the beginning, he enjoyed finding her there. In the first years of their marriage, she unbuttoned his stiff blue shirt and threw each side of it over his shoulders until it slid down his arms to hit the floor. Her hands were suddenly upon his chest, running over his belly, light and cool as a thin rain. She kissed him, bit his lips with her straight white teeth. She unlatched the top button of his workpants. She slowly let down his zipper, knelt and grabbed hunks of fabric at his hips to slide his pants down about his ankles. He lifted one foot at a time while she pulled off the pants and threw them into a clump in the middle of the porch. Coal dust tinkled against the wood like big grains of salt. As she stood, she ran her hands up the insides of his thighs and her lips were upon his again.

Back then on Fridays she had always worn outfits that were easily shed. One slick motion of his hand and thin cotton dresses simply fell away. Sometimes they sank down right there on the back porch and other times she led him into the house. He always liked watching her walk naked in front of him.

But after five years, this hardly ever happens anymore. Now it is just a chore they go through. She stands before him like a prison warden, watching him undress without any change of expression on her face. It seems as if she does not even remember how she once relished the smell of dirt and rock and coal dust on his skin, how his mouth was always as cold as the coal mine he had only recently left. She stands there with a hand out, waiting to take the pants and the shirt. She always says, "Put your socks down into your work-boots," like he is a little child.

Today he undresses, feeling as if he is doing so obediently. She throws his clothes into a cardboard box sitting near the door and says, "Throw your shorts in there, too, honey," and walks away. From inside she calls, "Supper'll be ready by the time you get out of the bathtub."

Adam pulls off his underwear and stands there naked. He is white and clean except for his face and arms, which are black and gritty. The summer air feels good on his cool skin. He stretches, listens to his bones pop. Their house sits so close to the high black mountain that nobody has a view of their back porch. The trees bend close, their leaves the color of limes. A breeze drifts through, no stronger than a breath. He smells sulfur seeping out of the cliffs way up on the mountainside. Birds call to one another. He considers the thick forest on the mountain, and wonders what all is stirring up in there.

Used to, he and Rita would have been making love under the warm leaves, in that summer air. If not that, they would have at least sat down—Rita on the second step, he in one of the mismatched assortment of chairs—and looked at the end of the day. She would have peeled potatoes and her laughter would have sung against the hidden cliffs. They would have talked about their day, made plans for Saturday night. They would have done at least that.

He goes into the house, leaving the door open behind him. She sighs with exaggeration and rushes from the kitchen to close it. He walks down the hallway and steps into the shower, using the hottest water he can stand. Steam pumps out and clouds the mirrors. He stands in the water for a long time, finally leaning his head against the wall and watching coal dust gather around the drain before it is sucked away.

*

He comes to the table clad only in his jeans. Beads of water stand on his freckled shoulders. The scent of his soap nearly overpowers that of the steaming food, which expels thin mists from each skillet and saucepan. Only when he sits down does he realize how tired he is.

Rita slices a tomato and spreads it out on a plate which is already full of fresh cucumbers, then douses it all with salt. She knows how to work a knife; each slice is the same thickness.

"Bad day?" she asks.

"Same as always," he says, and fills his mouth with

beans. They taste the way the garden smells when dew settles on the vines. He talks around them: "What'd you do today?"

"Cleaned about all day. Picked a big mess of beans. I was hoping you'd help me string the rest of them after while, if you feel like it."

"Why yeah," he says. He has always enjoyed breaking beans. He likes the sound of them, popping sharply as twilight settles itself out over the mountains.

"It'll be something to do, anyway," Rita says.

She is right, and he wonders if she meant to say this aloud. Every evening they look for something to do, to occupy their time. Their house is too quiet when night sets in. Adam has gotten to the point where he cannot stomach television. The garden has been hoed, the yard mown. The beans will be a way to pass the time before they go to bed and sleep with their backs facing.

Silverware chatters between them, a sound Adam despises. Outside, the porch chimes knock against one another briefly. He hopes that a rainstorm might be blowing in.

"We ought to just load up and go for a ride this evening," he says. He pops a couple of cucumbers into his mouth and works their green flavor around on his tongue. "Looks like it might cool off. Wouldn't it be a good night just to get out with the windows down?"

He can picture them, letting their hands float up and down against the speeding air, the smell of Rita's peach shampoo swirling around the cab of his truck. When the rain starts to fall, they will lean their faces out and let it touch them.

"Where would we go?" Rita says, with a crooked little

smile. "Ain't nothing to see."

He does not reply. It is so quiet that he imagines he can hear the salt sizzling into the meat of the tomatoes.

*

Rita places a large bowl on the floor between them and gives Adam a sheet of newspaper to spread across his lap. The beans lie clumped in a half-bushel basket, crowded together like skinny, living things. By the time he has strung one bean, she has gone through a handful. Already their curly strings litter the surface of her newspaper. She breaks them perfectly, each one snapping out four singular pops. When a bean is broken, she throws her hand into the air carelessly and the pieces fall into the bowl like green knuckles.

This was why he had first loved her. As a young girl, she watched carefully when her father showed her how to raise a garden. She kept her eyes on his hands, studied the way the seeds were tucked into the rows before they were covered, memorized the way he gripped the hoe-handle. Rita listened when her mother told her how to boil the jar-lids, how to add the canning salts atop the beans. She had been so beautiful in that special way girls of her raising have—always so clean, so fresh that she smelled as if she had stood out in the sun to dry herself right alongside her clothes. He had fallen for her because she was tough and strong, yet delicate and new at once. He had liked watching her deliberate, quick movements.

The cool of the day spreads itself out over them like slow water. Not long ago, the silence between them during such a chore would have been charming to Adam. But now the silence means something else.

The sound of children's laughter floats over from their neighbors' house. It seems that there is always a whole gang of children over there. Their own three, along with cousins and friends. They play out in the yard every evening, relishing the last days of summer. Adam imagines the neighbors are a family that never has problems or fights; their laughter seems that genuine.

"Listen to them kids," he says.

"What?"

"They're having a big time. Makes me feel old, don't it you? I feel like an old man, and I ain't even thirty yet."

"You're plenty young," she says, her eyes upon her work.

"That ain't what I mean." He hates it that she never picks up on his hints anymore. Used to, she could tell what he meant just by the tone of his voice. He is mad because she never wants to just jump up and do something for the pure hell of it. "I don't have fun like I did when I was a child. I miss that, being happy ever minute of the day. Not having a worry in the world. Being free."

"What worry do you have? You got this fine house, a good-paying job. We're doing good, got anything a person could want."

"Except a baby," he says. Finally he has said it, after all this time. Even though he has run these words over the back of his teeth a hundred times before, they still come out sounding wrong.

The quickening snap of beans is her only reply.

"I believe when you start to lose that childish feeling, you're meant to have a child to bring it back to you." He wants to smooth over this hole he has ripped in the air between them, but still she does not respond. "This house is too quiet, Rita. I can't stand it."

The chimes sing again. Leaves rub together like rough things, scratchy as sandpaper. The corner of Rita's newspaper stands straight up for a second, then settles again.

"Well, what do you want me to do about it, Adam? It's the way I'm made. There ain't nothing I can do about it."

"We could adopt a baby. Why not do that?"

Her hands become still in her lap. "Don't start on that again, now."

"We could keep trying. God knows all things."

"Does He, now?" She runs her tongue along the inside of her cheek and begins to break the beans again. Her face takes on a square shape. "I guess He knowed better than to give us a child, then, because that's exactly what He's done."

"Well, we might be meant to adopt one. I don't understand why you won't even talk about that," he says. "There's plenty of little children that needs a home."

"It's not that simple, though, Adam. You know that."

Adam sits up very straight in his chair to relieve the dull thud in the small of his back. Over in the neighbor's yard, the woman calls for the children not to get in the creek. He wonders if the neighbors sleep with their baby, as he and Rita had intended to do with their own. He thinks of how it would feel to lie down with such a little thing, to have your child curl up against you, her breath smelling like buttermilk as it played against your face.

"Ever since they told us we couldn't have a baby, we've grown further and further away from each other."

"Not we couldn't have one, Adam. *Me. I* couldn't have one."

"I'm not blaming you, Rita, and you damn-well know it."

"Sometimes I don't know."

He stands and leans against the porch rail. If he stops this now, she won't say another word. She is the silent one, the one who never looks him in the eye when they argue. He imagines that she tucks all of her feelings away in that place where the baby is meant to grow.

The air is still now. Frogs and cicadas begin to sing quietly, as if rehearsing. The rain has passed them by, but he can smell that it has fallen elsewhere. Before him the mountain stands blue and hunch-backed. He can feel animal eyes upon them.

"Have you give up?" he asks.

The newspaper in her lap crunches as she wads it up. She goes to the edge of the porch, lets the paper burst open, and the strings rain down upon the yard. Half of the beans are left, but she is finished.

"Answer me," he says.

She wraps her hands around the rail, holding it so tightly that Adam thinks she is afraid she might fall off. "Give up on us, or a baby?"

"Both," he says, and she makes no reply.

The first time she got pregnant, they both went a little wild. By Rita's first appointment with the doctor, they had already been to town to look at things for the nursery and picked out a name. After that doctor visit, he built the porch. He was no carpenter, but it turned out good. With the pounding of each nail a secret hope festered. He daydreamed of bringing his child out here on summer evenings just like this. He imagined dancing the baby to sleep, running his bristly chin across its thin hair. He planted ivy around the porch's legs and hung chimes from the roof's rafters. All of this for the baby that never came.

He blamed her for a little while, even though he had

not wanted to. During the first pregnancy, when the doctor told her she had a weak cervix and ordered her to complete bed-rest, he often came home to find the clothesline stretched tight with damp laundry, fresh dirt on the hoe he left propped against the porch. "I'll sure die if I just lay in the bed all day," she'd say. She miscarried twice more before the doctor told them that she would never be able to carry a child.

He carried the guilt of blaming her for a long time before letting it burn away. He knew that it was not her fault, but would never be able to convince her of this. Once something crept into her mind, it curled up and stayed there for good.

"If you don't want to try no more, at least break this silence," he says. "At least give me that."

"It's not me you want to hear talking."

"I want us to have a child, Rita. I don't care how."

Adam watches her for a long moment. She stares straight ahead, looking out so intently that it seems she is seeing something on the mountain that she has not noticed before. She is still holding onto the porch rail as if they stand on the bow of a great ship. "You think this distance between us can be fixed by bringing a baby to this house," she says. "A baby ain't no cure for something spoiled, Adam."

"It's not having it that stands between us."

"How can you be so sure? Lots of people have children and still drift apart. A child don't fix that."

"That ain't our situation," he says—almost a whisper. "I've loved you since junior high, Rita. It was only after we seen that a baby wouldn't be coming that things went wrong."

"I don't know how to please you no more. That don't have a thing to do with a child."

"You feel like I think less of you because we can't have a baby. That's what stands between us."

"No," she says, loudly, "I feel like I have to make it up to you for not being whole."

He doesn't know how to reply to this, so he decides he will pull her to him and this will let her know—finally—that she's wrong, that he doesn't blame her, that he wants the shards of this broken thing between them to fall back into place. She will feel the muscles of his arms encircling her, his breathing against her own chest, and know that he loves her. He tries to put his arm around her, but she pulls away.

She laughs beneath her breath. "I won't welcome no baby until this marriage is fixed, Adam. The baby won't do it for us."

"What will, then, Rita?" he asks. He curls his fingers into his palms, pounding his fists against the porch rail. "What am I supposed to do for you?"

He hardly ever raises his voices, but she does not seem taken aback by this. His shouting seems to strengthen her, to make her stubbornness more powerful.

"I don't know. Keep asking God, Adam." She spits out her words. Her face is altogether different, her lips pulled tight against her teeth. She looks as if another person has emerged beneath her skin. "You believe He can fix broken things. Or accept it and go on. That's the only two choices you have."

She turns and goes into the house, slamming the door. Her absence seems a more solid thing than her presence had been only moments before.

Adam can hear her running water inside the house.

Probably drawing a bath, he thinks. She always gets into the tub when she is aggravated. She has some candles on a little table near the tub and seems to think that their glow and the hot water will make her feel better. He wishes that he had never stopped smoking. Times like these he would have sucked on a cigarette as if it was a saving thing, relishing the sound of crackling tobacco, appreciating the angry dot of red near his mouth.

He watches the mountain. For just a moment it is that time when there is no day and no night, as if the whole world is holding its breath. Then, suddenly, darkness soaks up the air, like paint running over the sky. He waits for a long time, sitting there on the porch. He waits until the cries of crickets and katydids are nearly deafening, until the children next door have been ordered to come in. Lightning bugs hover near his face.

He sits there on his porch, waiting for her, but even after it is so dark that he can't tell the mountain from the sky, she still does not come out. All she has to do is step out onto the porch, put her hand on his arm. Used to be when they got into a fight, they made up quickly. They had a little unwritten treaty saying they wouldn't let sleep come before they reconciled. She would sometimes curl up right on his lap, her arms wrapped about his neck. If only she would do that tonight, everything would be fine. He would put his face into her hair and breathe in her good clean scent and they would begin to stitch their lives back together again. She wouldn't have to say anything. Just sit there and consider the summer night with him, let him know that she cares about the way he feels. But she doesn't.

He goes to his truck and backs out of the driveway, eases down the rough road. All down the holler, living room windows are blue with television glow. He crosses the bridge and is on the highway. He snaps on the radio, but finding no music that matches his mood, he turns it off so roughly that the knob tumbles into the floor. Once the warm air begins to slide into the cab of his truck, he puts his hand out and lets the wind run through his fingers.

He knows that there are only two things for him to do: leave her or keep living like this. He feels a sudden pang at the thought of her being alone. He can picture her, sitting in the bathtub, the room dark except for the flicker of short candles, her face flat and determined, unstained by tears. Still, he doesn't turn around. He will drive to wherever the rain has fallen and by then he will know what to do. When he finds that place where the highway has been made more black by the recent shower, where single drops of water roll down leaves every now and then, he will turn around and know what he has to do.

HANDCUFFED
Bev Marshall

She was weeding the zinnias along the split-rail fence when she first sensed his presence. The duck she'd named Matilda, with eight ducklings tumbling behind her, had just cut across the lawn on her way to the stream below the flowerbed. When Virginia lifted her eyes to the unfinished house next door, she saw him lounging against the framed back door. Tall. Broad. Powerful. He wore his work clothes like a tuxedo. His full-lipped mouth was curved into a smile, and when she bent forward in her white shorts to retrieve her trowel, she felt his eyes stalking her. As she reached behind her, tugging at her shorts, a low-pitched whistle soared through the light morning breeze. Blushing, she ripped off her gloves, scrambled to her feet, and hurried across the yard into her house.

The French colonial was new as were most of the houses in this newly developed subdivision in Madison, Mississippi. Virginia and Robert had moved here in the spring, and now in July, four more houses, filled with large families, had been built on their street. They had been married for nearly five years and did not plan to have children because they worried about overpopulation, the ozone layer, deforestation, pollution, terrorism, and as yet unnamed disasters Robert predicted would occur. Unlike many couples they knew, they had no financial worries. After graduating from Mississippi State College, both Virginia and Robert had landed good positions at Dermont Industries, Robert in the accounting department and she in public relations. Two weeks earlier Virginia had taken a leave of absence from Dermont and, although she had written "Health-related problems" on her request form, she had never felt more healthy. The truth was Virginia wanted time alone to assess the market value of her life. She knew that she owned the life that many women would bid for; she had everything they dreamed of: a prince charming, a beautiful home, an interesting job, friends, and youthful beauty that wouldn't fade for many years. She knew that she should be happy, but she couldn't make herself believe in the model for happiness she had created.

Robert was happy. Happy with the mold he had shaped for himself. He, who had pursued her through high school and college like a bloodhound on the scent of his prey, had in the last year metamorphosed into a poodle —high-strung, incessantly active, and vain to the point of getting veneers put on his nearly perfect teeth. Virginia was spending some of her alone time thinking about Robert's teeth.

But today, as she tidied the kitchen, her thoughts focused on the workman in the house next door. Each time she passed the gold-rimmed mirror hanging in the downstairs hall, pictures of his broad shoulders reappeared, and wandering through the silent rooms of her house, the resonance of his low-pitched whistle echoed in her head.

Tonight as she began dressing for a party at the Feldman's, she imagined his dark eyes watching her as she stepped into her panties, fastened her bra, slid silk stockings up her outstretched legs.

Robert threw his tie on the white satin bedspread and walked over to the closet where Virginia stood gazing at an array of expensive dresses she could no longer remember buying. "I've asked you twice. Where are my pearl cufflinks? What the hell are you thinking about?"

Virginia turned to him with a saucy smile. "Sex," she said. "Let's skip the party and stay home tonight." She pulled down the straps of her black lace bra and shimmied her shoulders. "Want to?"

"You know we're committed to go. Feldman does a lot of business with Dermont. Now get dressed." Snatching his tie from the bed and whipping it like a lasso around his thin neck, he turned to the mirror to fashion a perfect knot beneath his smooth-shaven chin.

After the party, which ended early because nearly everyone had to work the next day, Virginia peeled off her blue cocktail dress and new underthings and stepped into the double shower. She twisted the gold faucets on each end, and beneath the twin streams of hot water, she caressed her breasts in the rising steam. She felt the workman's dark eyes watching as she lathered her body. He was behind her, his arms around her shoulders, her hands were his, and she leaned backwards to lift her face to his lips.

She slept badly. In her cyclonic dreams she twisted the covers into funnels while Robert slept peacefully on his back, hands folded over his striped pajamas. Just before dawn, Matilda squawked loudly.

In the photograph in the morning paper, he looked older than twenty-two. The name of the man in the unfinished house was Eddie Lamont, and he had escaped from Parchman, the state prison. When he was eighteen, he had raped two women.

Shivering in her thin nightgown, Virginia pushed the newspaper across the maple breakfast table and pointed at the photograph. "I saw him. He was watching me from the Neales' new house. I thought he was a workman."

Robert bent his head to the paper. "Are you sure this is him?"

"Yes. Very sure."

Robert stood, went to the sink, and set his coffee mug into the metal basin. "Good Lord! Well, he won't hang around here. Probably over in Louisiana by now."

Before Robert left for work, Virginia followed him down the entry hall. "Robbbbert," she murmured. "Don't go. Stay home with me today." She pressed the length of her body against his brown suit.

He brushed past her. "You know I've got to get to work. What's the matter with you? You ought to get back to the office yourself. This taking a leave of absence doesn't make any sense at all." Before she could respond, he slammed the door against the morning sunlight.

In the dark living room Virginia moved to the front window, watched him stow his briefcase on the passenger seat, adjust his tie in the rear view mirror before shifting into reverse and carefully backing his immaculate Lincoln down the drive. Red brake lights blinked when the car reached the corner, and then he was gone.

Virginia walked back down the hall to the family

room. Without opening the drapes or turning on the light, she sat in Robert's black leather recliner. Aiming the remote control at the television set, she flipped through the channels. The same photograph she'd seen in the paper covered the screen on channel nine. Virginia pressed the volume button higher. ". . . served four years of his sentence before his escape. It is believed he may still be in the area." The picture was replaced with one of the mayor standing on the steps of city hall.

After shutting off the set, Virginia lifted the telephone receiver from the end table beside her and dialed her sister's number.

"Hello." Jan sounded grumpy and half-asleep.

"Hi! It's me. Did you watch the news this morning?"

"No, you woke me up. Call back after I've had my coffee."

Virginia twisted the cord around her index finger. "No. Wait. I just wanted to tell you that this convict escaped from Parchman. Eddie. And I saw him yesterday."

"Really?" Jan sounded more awake now. "What did he do?"

"You won't believe it. Rape. Two women." Saying the words, she felt a small thrill pass through her body. She gripped the receiver, wiggled her toes and bumped her heels against the chair. "And he was staring right at me from the Neales' house next door."

Jan's questions flew through the line, her voice filled with both horror and delight. Usually, Jan was the one who called Virginia with sensational stories about the colorful people who passed in and out of her life like seasonal storms. Two years older, but still single and living in a soon-to-be-condemned apartment building, Jan attracted chaos and reveled in it. She had always known what being happy meant to her.

While she hung on the phone, waiting for Jan to make coffee, Virginia pushed the recliner back and crossed her ankles on the leather footrest. She thought back to the conversation she'd had with her sister last week. She had told Jan she was thinking of seeing a therapist. Jan had snorted and said, "Save your money. Have an affair with someone who doesn't wear brown suits." Virginia had defended Robert by saying the same things she always said to Jan, who never missed an opportunity to express her dislike of him. "Robert is solid. Dependable. He makes me feel safe." Safe from what? She wondered now.

Jan had stolen the morning newspaper from her neighbor's doormat while waiting for the coffee to brew. She told her that Eddie Lamont was a hunk and said his eyes were hypnotic. "I can't imagine why he would have to rape to get some," she said. Then she advised Virginia to keep her doors locked and her drapes closed. "He could still be around, you know."

Later that morning Virginia, wearing black shorts and a white T-shirt, wandered through the professionally decorated rooms of her house. Robert liked symmetry, and now Virginia noticed that she had obediently decorated the house in pairs. Two end tables beside the green velvet couch, two pictures of fall landscapes perfectly aligned over it. Twin brass lamps, two campaign chests beside their lacquered Chinese bed.

Closing the drapes in the bedroom, Virginia stretched out on the satin comforter. She imagined a mirrored ceiling over the bed like the one she'd seen in their hotel room in Las Vegas when she and Robert had flown there for a company conference. She smiled up at her imaginary mirror. She stretched her legs out, curving her back into poses like those she'd seen in her brother's men's magazines. She closed her eyes. A dark figure appeared in the doorway; slowly he crossed the room to stand at the edge of the bed. Panther eyes stared down at their prey. Holding her breath, she waited. He bent forward, his hands encircled her wrists like handcuffs, and he lifted his knee to the space between her thighs, nudging her legs apart. She felt the weight of his chest pressing down against her breasts, and she struggled in his grip, arching her back, pushing harder against his body. He brought his lips to her ear, whispered her name. She shivered and then screamed out into the empty bedroom.

Her eyes flew open. She sprang up from the bed and pressed her palms to her hot cheeks. After splashing cold water on her face in the bathroom, she plummeted down the stairs to the family room, and yanking open the French doors, she burst out into the sunlit back yard.

On her knees in the flower bed, she jerked the Johnson grass from the warm earth. She had forgotten her gardening gloves. Dark soil collected beneath her nails and around her cuticles as she tore out the roots of the weeds and snapped wilted blooms from the plants. She rocked back on her heels and looking across the lawn, she saw Matilda waddling by, quacking to the little ones behind her. There were only seven of them now.

Virginia glanced over at the unfinished house. No workmen were there today. Rising to her feet, she crossed the yard to the Neales' house. Stepping through the framed walls of the open-air rooms, she peered behind the stacks of sheetrock, over the rolls of pink insulation. She turned toward the kitchen and walked to the framed double window. Her hands closed over the copper pipes sticking out of the wall. Lena Neale would stand here, washing dishes, listening to the laughter of her four children as they ran through the cluttered rooms of this house. She walked away to stand where Eddie had appeared the day before. Staring across the yard, she saw herself as he had seen her. On her knees in white shorts, yellow T-shirt stretched across her breasts, her long brown hair lifting in the breeze, she bent forward, serving up half moons of white flesh for his appetite. She bit her bottom lip and jumped down to the saw-dusted ground. Robert was right. Something *was* the matter with her.

In her pickle-wood kitchen Virginia reopened the newspaper and spread it across the table. She stared into Eddie's dark eyes, and with her dirty fingernail, she traced the outline of his unsmiling lips.

Around five o'clock a light rain began to fall. Blue and white police cars cruised the wet streets of the elegant neighborhood. Virginia sat in the wing chair beside the window staring out into the fading light. She felt his presence. His dark hair would be glistening with raindrops. His damp work clothes would cling to his broad back. He was only twenty-two; the same age she had been when she married Robert.

After she heard Robert's car pull into the drive, several minutes passed before he entered the house. When she met him in the kitchen, wet and angry, he threw his briefcase on top of the open newspaper. "I talked to the cops just now. They say that convict is still in the area. Someone saw him around five o'clock, just a couple of streets from here, on Elizabeth Drive. Stupid bastard."

"Still here?" she said with feigned surprise in her voice. Hadn't she sensed he was somewhere close by?

She watched Robert loosen his tie, shrug off his coat. He would go to the bar now to pour the single malt scotch into a glass jigger, measure just the right amount, before dumping it into a highball glass. Virginia smiled, anticipating his confusion when he couldn't find the jigger she'd hidden beneath the bar.

Virginia turned her head to the kitchen window where across the lawn in the mist he rose up like an apparition. With his body bent slightly forward, he jogged at a steady pace beside the stream. He halted beside the bank, knelt down, and scooped water into his mouth. "It's him!" She called out.

Robert wheeled around and ran toward her. "It's him? Son of a bitch!" He grabbed a knife from the wooden block beside the sink and raced toward the French doors.

He would hurt him. Kill him if he could. "NO," she screamed. And she was after him.

Robert's leather-soled shoes slid on the wet grass and, losing his balance, he landed face down in the zinnia bed. Leaping over him, Virginia trampled golden flowers and ran on toward the stream. It was raining harder now, and just ahead of her, Eddie loped with bent head, his uneven stride showing his fatigue. Before she reached him, an athletic-looking black policeman appeared from between two houses and gave chase. When she caught up to them in the Wagners' back yard, she saw the policeman with drawn gun standing over Eddie lying face down on the wet grass. As another policeman ran up and jerked Eddie's arms behind him, clamping the metal circles of the heavy steel handcuffs around his wrists, Virginia felt the weight of them dragging her own arms down to her sides. After they yanked Eddie to his feet, his eyes locked with hers. The predatory, stalking eyes had turned into two dark, empty hollows, and the full lips she had imagined against hers were tight white slashes across his handsome face. Virginia shivered and her hand stretched out in the empty space between them. The tips of her fingers brushed his chest for a brief moment before the black policeman pulled Eddie backwards. "Get back, lady. This man is dangerous," he shouted at her.

Virginia nodded acquiescence, but she knew the danger was past now. And she felt the same peculiar sense of loss she had experienced after last year's tornado had lifted before reaching her office building. She had been standing beside the window looking out at the funnel cloud sweeping across the sky, and she had felt an emptiness within that brought a sorrow so deep she had cried out to be released from the stone walls of the building that enclosed her.

Robert, knife dangling in his hand, limped up to her. Wordlessly, they watched as the policemen shoved Eddie across the lawn toward the patrol car. Robert grabbed her chin, forcing her face close to his. His flat, dull eyes stared into hers. "You're crazy," he said in a low voice filled with disgust. "You and your sister. You both ought to be locked up."

Virginia held his gaze. "I am locked up," she said. "But I'm going to escape."

"What's that supposed to mean?" He threw the knife on the ground between them. "Never mind. I'm going home. You should too," he said.

She waited until Robert reached the stream and turned toward their house, then stepped over the shining wet blade and marched toward the flashing lights of the patrol cars parked on the street. From the sidewalk, she watched the policemen shove Eddie into the back seat of the nearest car. When he turned his face to the rain-streaked window, she raised her open palm. His lips spread into a half-smile before he bowed his head. Crossing her arms over her chest, Virginia held on to her body, and pressing her lips together, she stifled the moan that rose up within her. Just before the patrol car pulled away from the curb, Virginia heard a faint, low-pitched whistle. But as she walked home beneath clearing skies, she thought that perhaps it was only the wind.

THE SECRET LIFE OF EMILY DOOLEY
Frank Turner Hollon

Emily Dooley was a twenty-three-year-old stripper. She was
good at it. Always smiled while she danced, standing up,
turning around, bending over looking between her open
legs, her brown hair hanging down, a hand on each of her
ass cheeks, dollar bills scattered around her high-heeled
shoes. She had become morally unhinged. No longer able
to separate right from wrong, and too busy to try.

"Why would a man want to sit there and just stare at my
privates?" she would say. Not just one man, one demented,
lonely, nasty man with a glass eye and greasy hair, but seemingly every man. Married men. College boys. Old grandpas
with chicken necks. They gathered around the stage
drinking overpriced watered-down bourbon and coke.

All she had to do was pick one out, look in his direction a few extra times, and the stupid bastard would
believe he was special. The trick was to pick out the guys
willing to pay for the attention. The guys who would hand
out crisp ten- and twenty-dollar bills instead of balled-up
moist one-dollar bills tossed on the stage like peanuts to a
monkey.

Fat guys were usually good. They didn't get much attention in the real world. They were willing to pay for the things that good-looking guys got for free. Sometimes they would close their eyes during a lap dance and Emily would wonder what they were thinking about. She felt no guilt when she threw away the little pieces of paper with the phone numbers scrawled in blue ink. Her dance name was Vanessa. They all called her Vanessa. It was just a name she always liked.

Working at the club was more than a job. It was a way of life. A way of life almost everyone there said they hated, but almost no one left. The money was too easy. What could be easier than being paid to be looked at? Just stand up, take off your clothes, wiggle around, and stick the cash in your pocket at 3 a.m. The girls talked about saving money and going to college. But nobody saved any money, and nobody went to college. They just got drunk for free, danced naked, and rubbed their bare asses into the crotches of strangers. Complete strangers who paid money to simulate intimate acts with other strangers with fake names.

There were always regulars, of course. Men who would ask about the weekly schedule and come on a particular night for a particular girl. Vanessa would talk to some of these men like real people, but she was very careful not to become friends. A man desperate enough to seek friendship with a stripper is not a man to be trusted, Emily believed.

She kept herself clean and exercised at the gym three times a week. Everything was the same until the day she fell in love with Austin McAdoo.

Austin McAdoo. Three hundred forty-seven pounds. Six feet four, three hundred forty-seven pounds, not an ounce of muscle. He had his pants specially made. He wasn't particularly friendly, and was born with a small sense of humor, although he was a huge fan of the Three Stooges.

Austin McAdoo came into the club on a Thursday night. He was a businessman staying at the hotel down the avenue, looking for a place to have a drink. He had no idea it was a strip joint until he had already found a seat at the bar and ordered a milk punch. Austin McAdoo turned his head around to the stage, locked eyes with naked Vanessa, and turned back to his milk punch like nothing happened. In fact, he sat at the bar for thirty minutes and never turned his head again.

It was a slow night. Vanessa was intrigued by the well-dressed fat man, an obvious target from across the room. She sat down next to him at the bar. Austin McAdoo, with his jet black hair and walnut eyes, turned to Vanessa and said, "No time for whores."

His head was large like a melon. His eyebrows were thick and bushy. He stuck his tongue out slightly into the glass held to his lips, touching the cold ice cubes with his red, meaty cow tongue. Emily was amazed by his massive features.

Softly she said, "Please don't call me a whore."

Austin McAdoo swivelled his melon head back toward the girl. With his sausage-like fingers he picked up a nickel from the bar.

"Do you see this nickel?"

"Yes," Emily answered.

"I'll give you one hundred dollars to put this nickel in your ass. One hundred dollars. You have to leave it there for five minutes."

Emily looked at the nickel held between the fat fingers. It looked so small in comparison to the big white thumbnail. She thought about the question.

"Are you some type of giant?" Emily asked. She was naked from the waist up. Her well-formed tan breasts went unnoticed.

"Don't change the subject. Yes or no? Nickel in the ass for five minutes, one hundred dollars. No nickel in the ass for five minutes, no one hundred dollars. Can your mouse-sized brain hold the question long enough to make a decision? Yes or no? Would you like to see the one hundred dollars? Laboratory rats need to see the prize before they gnaw off their own teats."

It was a slow night. Emily could use the one hundred dollars. She pondered the specifics of the question, and then noticed the ears on Austin McAdoo. They were the size of China tea saucers. Much like a regular ear, except bigger. Emily Dooley felt a lightness. It was wonderful and odd at the same time. She saw herself having the children of the enormous man holding the nickel.

People talk about love at first sight. It's been written about since the beginning of time. It's very rare, but it does happen. And when it happens, there are no boundaries. The rules of gravity no longer apply. Physics is useless. Vanessa, Emily, whatever the hell her name was, felt herself pulled into orbit around Austin McAdoo, the largest man she had ever seen.

Emily said, "If I put that nickel in my ass for one hundred dollars, then I guess I'm just a whore like you said. But if *I* give *you* one hundred dollars for that nickel, and then I put the nickel in my ass anyway, then I guess you'll feel like a fool."

Austin McAdoo followed the words. He squinted his

eyes as if to size up the person in the chair next to him that he hadn't really noticed before. His eyes glanced down to her naked breasts and then back up to the face.

"I guess you're right," he said, and then smiled. His mouth was the size of a horse's mouth, the teeth like big ivory chunks. Emily leaned over and kissed Austin McAdoo on the lips. It was the first time she'd kissed a man on the lips since Ernie Sullivan in high school.

It was soft. He was a delicate kisser. They both kept their eyes open, and Emily reached her hand up to the big man's cheek, touching his oily skin gently with her thin fingers like a butterfly. For a moment, they were weightless. He was not himself, and she was ready to leave.

The kiss ended.

Austin McAdoo said, "I was wondering, would you like to leave this place forever?"

"Yes. I would."

"Is there anything here you need to get?"

"No."

"Can you fit everything you need in a suitcase?"

"Maybe two suitcases," she said.

Austin McAdoo began the process of getting off his barstool. He used his arms to lift a portion of his weight from the chair and then pushed back slightly to gain some space in between. His incredible buttocks rose, and then he was standing. Emily caught the stool as it teetered and started to tip over. Austin McAdoo put the nickel in his pocket.

"You can stay with me this evening at the hotel. My room has two double beds. You should be quite comfortable. In the morning, we'll be leaving at 7 a.m. We can go to your place now to pack."

"O.K.," Emily said.

Austin removed his mammoth jacket from the back of the stool and draped it over Emily's shoulders as she turned around. He retrieved a large overstuffed wallet from his back pocket and left a crisp twenty-dollar bill on the bar. The large man turned and stood facing Emily. The bartender looked and then looked back again. It was like an optical illusion.

"What's your name?" Austin asked.

"Emily. Emily Dooley." She smiled. It felt good to say it out loud.

"What's your name?" Emily asked.

"Austin. Austin McAdoo."

"That's a good name," Emily said.

She put out her hand, and Austin McAdoo covered her hand with his. It was a perfect fit.

WATER DOG GOD
Brad Watson

Back in late May a tornado dropped screaming into the canyon. Trunks and limbs snapped loud as artillery rounds. Squirrels and birds shot through the black sky. And in the wet and quiet shambles after, several new stray dogs crept into the yard, and on their heels little Maeve. You've seen pictures of those children starving on TV, living in filthy huts and wearing rags and their legs and arms just knobby sticks, huge brown eyes looking up at you like you were from another planet. That's the closest I can come to what Maeve looked like.

These strays, I sometimes think there is something their bones are tuned to that draws them here, like the whistle only they can hear, or words of some language ordinary humans have never known—the language that came from Moses' burning bush, which only Moses could hear. I think sometimes I've heard it at dawn, something in the green, smoky air. Who knows what Maeve heard, maybe nothing but a big riproaring on the roof: the black sky opens up, she walks out. She follows an old coon dog along the path of forest wreckage through the hollow and into my yard, her belly huge beneath a sleeveless bit of cloth she called her nightslip.

I knew her as my Uncle Sebastian's youngest child, who wouldn't ever go out of her room, and here she was wandering in the woods. They lived up beyond the first dam, some three miles up the creek. She says to me, standing there holding a little stick she's picked up along the way, "I don't know where I'm at." She gives an absent whack at the hound. He's a bluetick with teats so saggy I thought him a bitch till I saw his old jalapeño.

I said, "Lift up that skirt and let me see you." I looked at her white stomach, big as a camel's hump and bald as my head, stretched veins like a map of the pale blue rivers of the world, rivers to nowhere. I saw her little patch of frazzly hair and sex like a busted lip wanting nothing but to drop the one she carried. Probably no one could bear to see it but God, after what all must have climbed onto her, old Uncle Sebastian and those younger boys of his, the ones still willing to haul pulpwood so he hadn't kicked them out on their own, akin to these stray dogs lying about the yard, no speech, no intelligent look in their eyes. This creature in Maeve would be something vile and sub-human.

Later on, when I figured it was near time for her to have the child, I told her the story of Sodom. I said some voice told her to leave, that something like an angel had led her away from her home, and she mustn't even look back. "It was just an old dog," she said, and kicked at the hound, still sniffing her up. I gave him a good one in the ribs and he hobble-hunched off. *He* was no angel, that's for sure, I'd seen him humping the old Snapper lawn-mower I hadn't cranked in four years.

I said, "The likes of those which have made your child, Maeve, should not be making babies, at least not with you. It was an evil thing that led to it."

She said, "Well, when the roof lifted off the house and blew away I climbed on out. They was all gone, out hiding or gone to town."

*

She took to wearing the little blue earphones radio I got in the mail with my Amoco card. I had no idea what she was listening to. She wandered around looking at nothing, one hand pressing a little speaker to an ear, the other aimless, signing. At some point you begin to pick things up—the burning bush, the voice of God walking in the Garden, calling, Maeve? Every sound that ever was is still a sound somewhere. It may be some can still hear the first sounds, they may eddy in a little canyon for a time. If you're listening and have switched off everything else you may hear it as it was, the muttering and cries and grumbling of the world's creation, the early confusion of sounds.

She would never even change out of her nightslip, though when I'd washed it for her it nearly fell apart. She was pale as a grub, hair a wet black rag all pressed to her head. Not even seventeen and small, but she looked old somehow, aged by experience if not by years. She'd seen so very little of the world and what she'd seen was scarcely human. She would forget or just not bother to use the toilet paper. Climb into the dry bathtub and fall into naps where she twitched like a dreaming dog. She heaved herself somehow up the ladder and through the little hole in the hallway ceiling and sat in the attic and bathed in her own sweat and came down wheezing from the insulation dust. Maybe the little fibers got into her brain and improved her reception.

I made her put on a raincoat over the nightslip and took her to the grocery store since I didn't want to leave her alone. I thought if I took her there she wouldn't think herself so strange compared to some of the women who lurk those aisles. Town is only three miles away but you would not think it to stand here and look at the steep green walls of the canyon. And what does it matter? The whole world, and maybe others, is in the satellite dish at the edge of the yard, and I have sat with Maeve until three in the morning watching movies, industrial videos, German game shows, Mexican soap operas. It's what Greta would do sometimes while she was dying, her body sifting little by little into the air. When I started to get the disability and was home all the time I could see this happening, so I wasn't surprised when one morning I woke and she didn't. I grieved but I wasn't surprised. She was all hollowed out. We'd never had a child as she was unable and near the end I think she believed her life had been for nothing. I felt the same way about myself after some twenty-odd years at ChemGlo. Sometimes it seems I wasn't even there in that job, I'd only dreamed up a vision of hell, a world of rusty green and leaky pipes and tanks and noxious fumes. When the boss said to make the illegal burn at 3 a.m. I made it, and the whole county woke up feeling like they'd inhaled battery acid. But as I was not there anymore and was not dead, I began to believe or hope my life might have some purpose, though nothing had happened to confirm that until Maeve appeared.

At the grocery store I couldn't get her away from the

produce section. She wouldn't put on any shoes, and she was standing there in her grimy, flat, skinny bare feet, the gray raincoat buttoned up to her chin, running her dirty little fingers all over the cabbages and carrot bunches, and when the nozzles shot a fine spray over the lettuce she stuck her head in there and turned her face up into the mist. I got her down to the meat and seafood area, where she stood and looked at the lobsters in their tank until I had everything else loaded into the cart, and I lured her to the cashier with a Snickers bar. She stood behind me in the line eating it while I loaded the groceries onto the conveyer belt, chocolate all over her mouth and her fingers, and she sucked on her fingers when she was done. And then she reached over to the little candy shelf in the cashier chute and got herself another one, opened it up and bit into it, as if this was a place you came to when you wanted to eat, just walked around in there seeing what you wanted and eating it.

"I believe she's craving a Snickers bar," said the cashier, a dumpy little blonde woman with a cute face whose name tag said Hi I'm Miranda your cashier today. So I just picked up the whole little box, what was left on the shelf, and laid them on the conveyer belt. Miranda smiled at Maeve and said, "Eating for two, huh!" and laughed. "I wish my husband was as sweet as yours." She winked. "I should of gotten *me* an older man." Maeve stopped chewing the Snickers and stared as if she'd never seen me before in her life.

*

Understand, we are in a wooded ravine, a green and jungly gash in the earth, surrounded by natural walls. This land between the old mines and town, it's wooded canyons cut by creeks that wind around and feed a chain of quiet little lakes on down to ours, where the water deepens, darkens, and pours over the spillway onto the slated shoals. From there it rounds a bend down toward the swamps, seeps back into the underground river. The cicadas spool up so loud you think there's a little torn seam in the air through which their shrieking slipped from another world. Hammerhead woodpeckers swoop through leaflanes, fix onto grub-eaten ash, and belt out their loud jungle calls. Coons and mink scoot along little trails and armadillos root in the rotten fallen trunks of trees. Screech owls rip the night into jagged halves.

One evening I was out on the porch in the late light after supper and saw Maeve sneak off into the woods. The coon dog got up and followed her, and then a couple of other strays followed him. When she didn't come right back I stood up and listened. The light was leaking fast into dusk. Crickets and treefrogs sang their high-pitched songs. Then from the woods in the direction she'd headed came a sudden jumble of high vicious mauling. It froze me to hear it. Then it all died down. I went inside for the shotgun and a light but when I came back out Maeve had made her way back through the thicket and into the ghostly yard, all color gone to shadowy gray, the nightslip wadded into a diaper she held to herself with both hands. I suppose it wasn't this child's first. She walked through the yard. What dogs hadn't gone with her stood around with heads held low, she something terrible and holy, lumpy stomach smeared with blood. She went to the lake to wash herself and the slip, soaking and wringing it till she fell out and I had to go save her and take her into the house and bathe her myself and put her to bed. Her swollen little-girl's bosoms were smooth and white as the moon, the leaky nipples big as berries. I fed her some antibiotics left over from when I'd had the flu, and in a short time she recovered. She was young. Her old coon hound never came back, nor the others that went out with him, and I had a vision of them all devouring one another like snakes, until they disappeared.

I couldn't sleep and went out into the yard, slipped out of my jeans and into the lake. I thought a swim might calm me. I was floating on my back in the shallows looking up at the moon so big and clear you could imagine how the dust would feel between your fingers. My blood was up. I thought I heard something through the water, and stood. It was coming from across the lake, in the thick bramble up on the steep ridge, where a strange woman had moved into an empty cabin some months back. I heard a man one night up there, howling and saying, maybe, her name, I couldn't tell what it was. I'd seen her in town. She carried herself like a man, with strong wiry arms, a sun-scored neck, and a face hard and strange as the wood knots the carvers call tree spirits. When I stood up in the water I could hear a steady rattling of branches and a skidding racket, something coming down the steep ridge wall. I waded back toward the bank, stopped and looked, and she crashed out of the bushes overhanging the water, dangling naked from a moonlit branch. She dropped into the lake with a quiet little splash, and when she entered the water it was like she'd taken hold of me. I didn't do that to myself anymore, though maybe I should've because I was sometimes all over Maeve in my sleep until she began to shout and scratch, for she was too afraid to sleep alone but must not be touched even by accident. But now here I was spilling myself into the shallows where the water tickled my ankles, my seed little rolling pearls snapped up by mudcats, bream, and yearling bass.

I saw her arms rise from the water and wheel slowly over her round wet head and dip again beneath. She made no noise. She swam around the curve up into the shallows and crawled toward me on all fours and never took her eyes off my own. She stood up, took my hand, and looked into the palm. She had a lean rangy skinned-cat body, a deep little muttering voice.

"Small slim hands," she said, "a sad and lonely man. You see the big picture, you have a vision. But you have no real life." She grumbled a minute. "Short thin fingers, tapered ends. A stiff and waisted thumb, hmmm. Better off alone, I suppose." She pressed into the flesh below my thumb. "Ummhmm," she said, tracing all the little cracks and stars and broken lines in the middle of the palm with a light fingernail. She looked at it close for a second, then dropped it. She turned and sighed and looked back across the lake. I turned my eyes from her saggy little fanny and skinny legs.

"My name's Callie, I'm your neighbor," she said.

"I know it," I said.

She said, "Who's that little girl you taking care of?"

"My niece," I said, though she was really just a younger cousin, but I had told her to call me uncle as it felt more natural. I said, "She's had a hard life."

"Mmm," she said, and we were quiet for a while. "Well the world ain't no place for an innocent soul, now is it?"

"It is not," I agreed.

"Must be hard on a man," she said.

"I don't know what you mean."

"I mean being alone out here with a pretty little girl."

"She's my niece, I'm not that way."

She turned and looked at me and then at the house for a minute.

"Why don't you come on up to the ridge sometime and pay me a visit?" Her thin lips crooked up and parted in a grin. She raised a hand and walked back into the water and swam around the curve into the cove and out of sight. I hear she's an installer for the phone company, and pretty good. I sat down on the bank. There was a sound and I turned my head to see Maeve standing unsteady on the porch, fiddling with something in her hands. It was the little blue headphones radio which she didn't at the moment seem to understand how to use. Then in a minute she had them on again, and just stood there.

Once Maeve put on those headphones, she scarcely ever took off, not even when she slept. So if she was quiet before, now with her head shot through with radio waves she was hardly more than a ghost. She ate raw peanuts from a sack I had on the kitchen counter, and drank her water from the lake, down on her hands and muddy knees. Now she wasn't carrying, she roamed the canyon with the strays. She smelled like a dog that's been wallowing in the lake mud, that sour dank stink of rotten roots and scum. I finally held her in the bathtub one day, took the headphones off her head and plunged her in, her scratching and screaming. I scrubbed her down and lathered up her head and dunked her till she was squeaky, and plucked a huge fat tick out of her scalp. But when I tried to dress her in some of Greta's old clothes, shut up in plastic and mothballs all these years, she slashed my cheek with her raggedy nails and ran through the house naked and making a high, thin, and breathless sound until she sniffed out the old rag she wore and flew out through the yard and into the woods buck naked with that rag in her hand and didn't come back till that evening, wearing it, smelling of the lake water again, and curled up asleep on the bare porchboards. When I went to the screen door she didn't look up but said from where she lay hugging herself, "Don't you handle me that way no more."

"I had to clean you, child."

"I can't be touched," she said.

*

I fixed her a makeshift bed on the sofa in the den where I finally convinced her to sleep. As long as I kept my distance and made no sudden moves toward her and did not ever raise my voice above the gentle words you would use with a baby, we were all right. But it was not a way any man could live for long and I wondered what I could do—send her back to Sebastian's place, where she was but chattel? I feared one day she would wander into the woods and go wild. I might have called the county, said, Look, this child, who has wandered here from my uncle's house, is in need of attention and there is nothing more I can do. Who would take in such a child but at the mental hospital up in Tuscaloosa, where she'd live among Queen Elizabeths and others who thought they were monkeys or Jesus?

I figured Sebastian thought she'd been sucked up into the twister and scattered into blood and dust, until the afternoon I heard his pickup muttering and coughing along the dam and then his springs sighing as he idled down the steep drive to the house, and then his creaking door and I was out on the porch waiting on him. He stopped at the steps and nodded and looked off across the lake as if we were lost together in thought. Uncle Sebastian was old and small and thin and hard as a scythe and he had the impish and shrewd face of all his siblings. His face was narrow and his eyes slanted down and in and his chin jutted up so that if you viewed him in profile his head was the blade of that scythe and his body the handle. He blinked in the sun and said, "We been most of the summer fixing up the house after that tornado back in the spring."

I said, "Anybody hurt?"

"Well we thought we'd lost little Maeve." And he turns to me. "Then I hear tell she's showed up over here, staying with you."

"Where would you hear that?" I said, and he said nothing but I saw his eyes shift just a fraction up toward the ridge where the crazy woman's house is perched and I thought, So.

The strays had shown little interest in Sebastian's arrival and kept mainly to their little scooped-out cool spots under the bushes, a flea-drowsing shade. Hardly moved all August, through the long hot days all you'd hear was the occasional creaking yawn, wet gnashing of grooming teeth, isolated flappity racket of a wet dog shaking out his coat. Hardly any barking at all. We heard a rustling and Maeve stood at the edge of the yard in her headphones, a scruffy little longhaired stray at her heels.

"She *was* with child," Sebastian said.

"She lost it."

"That late?" he said and looked at me a long moment, then back at Maeve. "You keeping her outdoors and living with dogs?"

"If it was true it would not be so different from what she came from," I said.

"Go to hell," Sebastian said. "Living out here by yourself, you going to tell me you ain't been trying some of that?"

"That's right."

"Them boys of mine done all wandered off now she's gone. I ain't got no help."

He walked slowly toward Maeve who was standing there with two fingers of one hand pressed to the little speaker over her right ear, head cocked, eyes cut left looking out at the lake. The little stray slinked back into the brush. Only when Sebastian laid his hand on Maeve's arm did she lean away, her bare feet planted the way an animal that does not want to be moved will do. He began to drag her and she struggled, making not a sound, still just listening. I walked up behind Sebastian and said his name, and when he turned I hit him between the eyes with the point of my knuckle. Small and old as he was, he crumpled. Maeve did not run then but walked over to the porch, up the steps, and into the house.

I dragged the old man by his armpits to the water, and waded out with him trailing. Maeve came out again and followed in her nightslip to the bank, and stood there eating a cherry popsicle. She took the popsicle out of her mouth and held it like a little beacon beside her head. Her lips were red and swollen-looking. She took the blue headphones off her ears and let them rest around her neck. I could hear the tinny sound of something in there, now it wasn't inside of her head.

"What you doing with that man?" she said.

"Nothing," I said.

"Are you drownden him?"

I said the first thing that came to mind.

"I am baptizing," I said. "I am cleansing his heart."

It was late afternoon then. I looked back over my shoulder at Maeve. She was half-lit by sunlight sifting through the leaves, half in shadow. A mostly naked child in a rotten garment. Underwater, Uncle Sebastian jerked and his eyes came open. I held him harder and waded out to where it was up to my shoulders and the current strong toward the spillway, my heart heavy in the water, the pressure there pressing on it. Behind me, Maeve waded into the shallows.

"I want it too, Uncle," she called.

Sebastian's arms ceased thrashing, and after a minute I let him go. I saw him turning away in the water. Palms of his hands, a glimpse of an eye, the ragged toe of a boot dimpling the surface, all in a slow drifting toward the spillway, and then gone in the murk. Maeve lifted the gauzy nightslip up over her head as she waded in, her pale middle lumpy and soft and mapped with squiggly brown stretch marks. I pushed against the current trying to reach her before she got in too deep. There was such unspeakable love in me. I was as vile as my uncle, as vile as he claimed.

"Hold still, wait there," I said at the very moment her head went under as if she'd been yanked from below. The bottom is slippery, there are uncounted little sinkholes. Out of her surprised little hand, the nightslip floated a ways and sank. I dove down but the weight of the water and something thick like fear or dread made me slow and I could not reach her. My eyes were open but the water was so muddy I could barely even see my own hands. I kept gasping up and diving down, the sun was sinking into the trees.

She would not show again until dusk, when from the bank I saw her ghost rise from the water and walk into the woods. The strays tuned up. There was a ringing from the telephone inside the house. It would ring and stop a while. Ring and then stop. The sheriff's squadron rolled its silent flickering way through the trees. Their lights put a flame in all the whispering leaves. There was a hollow taunting shout from up on the ridge but I paid it no mind.

I once heard at dawn the strangest bird, like one of those telephones with the ring that isn't a bell, some electronic underwater angel's song, and I went outside. It was coming from the east of the house in the woods, where the tornado would come through. I walked down a trail, looking up. It got louder. I got to where it had to be, it was all around me in the air, but there was nothing in the trees. A pocket of air had picked up a signal, the way a tooth filling will pick up a radio station. It rang in my blood, it and me the only living things in that patch of woods, all the creatures fled or dug in deep, and I remember that I felt a strange happiness.

Contributors

Authors

John T. Edge writes frequently for *Gourmet* and other publications. His work was featured in the 2001, 2002, and 2003 editions of the *Best Food Writing* compilation. Edge is at work on four books that examine iconic American foods. *Fried Chicken: An American Story* is the first. Edge holds a master's degree in Southern Studies from the University of Mississippi and is director of the Southern Foodways Alliance, an affiliated institute of the Center for the Study of Southern Culture at the University of Mississippi. He lives in Oxford, Mississippi, with his son, Jess, and his wife, Blair Hobbs, a poet and painter.

Beth Ann Fennelly teaches at the University of Mississippi and lives in Oxford. She has published two books, *Open House*, winner of the 2001 Kenyon Review Prize and the GLCA New Writers Award, and *Tender Hooks*, published by W. W. Norton in 2004. She was awarded an NEA grant in 2003.

Tom Franklin is the author of *Poachers*, a short story collection, and *Hell at the Breech*, a novel, both published by William Morrow. Recipient of a 2001 Guggenheim Fellowship, he teaches at the University of Mississippi, in Oxford, where he lives with his wife, poet Beth Ann Fennelly, and their young daughter, Claire.

Frank Turner Hollon is the author of four novels, *The Pains of April, The God File, A Thin Difference,* and *Life Is a Strange Place.* His novels have been selected by BookSense and Barnes and Noble's Discover Great New Writers Program. *The God File* was chosen as the independent publisher's novel of the year for 2002. Frank lives with his wife and family in Baldwin County, Alabama.

SILAS HOUSE is the author of *Clay's Quilt* and *A Parchment of Leaves*, a national bestseller. He is the winner of the Award for Special Achievement from the Fellowship of Southern Writers, the Kentucky Literary Award for Best Novel, and many other honors. Twice nominated for the Pushcart Prize, his short fiction has appeared in *Night Train, The Beloit Fiction Journal, The Louisville Review,* and other magazines. He serves as a contributing editor for *No Depression* magazine and frequently reads his short fiction on NPR's "All Things Considered." A graduate of the Spalding University MFA program, he lives in Eastern Kentucky with his wife and two daughters.

SUZANNE HUDSON's first novel, *In a Temple of Trees*, was published in 2003, and her second novel, *In the Dark of the Moon*, is due out this fall. A collection of short stories, *Opposable Thumbs*, which was a finalist for the John Gardner Fiction Book Award, was published in 2001. Her stories have appeared in Volumes I and II of *Stories from the Blue Moon Café*. She is a resident of Fairhope, Alabama, where she is a middle school guidance counselor and writing teacher.

MICHAEL KNIGHT has published a novel, *Divining Rod,* and two collections of short fiction, *Dogfight & Other Stories* and *Goodnight, Nobody*. He teaches creative writing at the University of Tennessee.

JAMIE KORNEGAY lives and writes in his native north Mississippi. He works at an independent bookstore in Oxford and serves as a producer for Thacker Mountain Radio.

BEV MARSHALL is the author of *Right as Rain* (Ballantine Books, 2004) and *Walking Through Shadows* (MacAdam/Cage, 2002). She grew up in McComb and Gulfport, Mississippi, and now lives in Ponchatoula, Louisiana, just down the road from a caged alligator that serves as the town's tourist attraction.

JENNIFER PADDOCK was born and raised in Fort Smith, Arkansas. "The Ones Who Are Holding Things Up" is from her novel *A Secret Word* (Touchstone/Simon & Schuster, 2004). A former resident of Fairhope, Alabama, she lives in New York City with her husband, Sidney Thompson.

RON RASH is the author of three books of poems, two story collections, and two novels. In 2002, his first novel, *One Foot in Eden*, was named Appalachian Book of the Year. His most recent novel is *Saints at the River* (Henry Holt, 2004). He teaches at Western Carolina University.

MICHELLE RICHMOND is the author of *Dream of the Blue Room* (2003), which was a finalist for the Northern California Book Award, and *The Girl in the Fall-Away Dress* (2001), which won the Associated Writing Programs Award for Short Fiction. A native of Alabama, she lives in Northern California and teaches writing at the University of San Francisco. She also edits the online literary journal *Fiction Attic*.

SIDNEY THOMPSON's stories have appeared in *The Southern Review*, *The Carolina Quarterly*, *Stories from the Blue Moon Café* Volumes I and II, among other publications. A former resident of Fairhope, Alabama, he lives in New York City with his wife, Jennifer Paddock.

BRAD WATSON is the author of *Last Days of the Dogmen* and *The Heaven of Mercury*, both from W.W. Norton & Co. "Water Dog God" first appeared in *The Oxford American*. He lives on the Alabama Gulf Coast and in Oxford, Mississippi, where he is the 2004–05 John and Renée Grisham Writer-in-Residence at Ole Miss.

STEVE YARBROUGH is the author of three short story collections and three novels, the most recent of which is *Prisoners of War*. A native of Indianola, Mississippi, he divides his time now between Fresno and Krakow.

Editors

WILLIAM GAY is the author of the novels *Provinces of Night* and *The Long Home* and of the short story collection *I Hate to See that Evening Sun Go Down.* He is the winner of the 1999 William Peden Award and the 1999 James A. Michener Memorial Prize and recipient of a 2002 Guggenheim fellowship. He lives in Hoenwald, Tennessee, where he is at work on his third novel.

SUZANNE KINGSBURY is the author of the novels *The Summer Fletcher Greel Loved Me* and *The Gospel According to Gracey.* She was born in Baltimore, Maryland. In 1999 she became a literary nomad, living and writing in Mississippi, Georgia, Arizona, Panama and Mexico. She currently resides in Brattleboro, Vermont, where she is at work on her third novel.